Hilary reached out for Matthew, and he took her hand.

"I'm so tired of talking, Matt. So tired of trying to figure things out."

"Amen to that. Even my scientist's brain has had enough of critical analysis." He drew her willingly into the circle of his arms and laid his cheek against her hair. For a long time, they stood like that, holding each other silently, breathing in unison. The greenhouse smelled of fertile soil and lush, burgeoning life.

When another gust of wind blew through the greenhouse, it brought more than rain with it. The damp air caressing Matt's skin touched off a flood of desire.

Suddenly nothing mattered but Hilary. He needed her. He desperately wanted the closeness making love to her would bring. If he didn't dare tell her the depth of his feelings, he could show her....

Dear Reader:

Happy July! It's a month for warm summer evenings, barbecues and—of course—the Fourth of July. It's a time of enjoyment and family gatherings. It's a time for romance!

The fireworks are sparkling this month at Silhouette Romance. Our DIAMOND JUBILEE title is *Borrowed Baby* by Marie Ferrarella, a heartwarming story about a brooding loner who suddenly becomes a father when his sister leaves him with a little bundle of joy! Then, next month, don't miss *Virgin Territory* by Suzanne Carey. Dedicated bachelor Phil Catterini is determined to protect the virtue of Crista O'Malley—and she's just as determined to change her status as "the last virgin in Chicago." Looks like his bachelorhood will need the protection instead as these two lovers go hand in hand into virgin territory.

The DIAMOND JUBILEE—Silhouette Romance's tenth anniversary celebration—is our way of saying thanks to you, our readers. To symbolize the timelessness of love, as well as the modern gift of the tenth anniversary, we're presenting readers with a DIAMOND JUBILEE Silhouette Romance title each month, penned by one of your favorite Silhouette Romance authors. In the coming months, writers such as Annette Broadrick, Lucy Gordon, Dixie Browning and Phyllis Halldorson are writing DIAMOND JUBILEE titles especially for you.

And that's not all! There are six books a month from Silhouette Romance—stories by wonderful authors who time and time again bring home the magic of love. During our anniversary year, each book is special and written with romance in mind. July brings you *Venus de Molly* by Peggy Webb—a sequel to her heartwarming *Harvey's Missing*. The second book in Laurie Paige's poignant duo, *Homeward Bound*, is coming your way in July. Don't miss *Home Fires Burning Bright*—Carson and Tess's story. And much-loved Diana Palmer has some special treats in store in the month ahead. Don't miss Diana's fortieth Silhouette—*Connal*. He's a LONG, TALL TEXAN out to lasso your heart, and he'll be available in August....

I hope you'll enjoy this book and all of the stories to come. Come home to romance—Silhouette Romance—for always!

Sincerely,

Tara Hughes Gavin
Senior Editor

KAREN LEABO

Full Bloom

Published by Silhouette Books New York
America's Publisher of Contemporary Romance

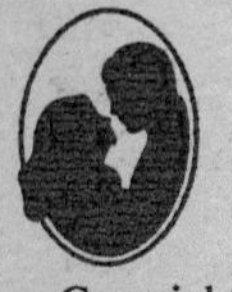

SILHOUETTE BOOKS
300 E. 42nd St., New York, N.Y. 10017

ISBN: 0-373-08731-4

First Silhouette Books printing July 1990

Printed in the U.S.A.

Books by Karen Leabo

Silhouette Romance

Roses Have Thorns #648
Ten Days in Paradise #692
Domestic Bliss #707
Full Bloom #731

KAREN LEABO

credits her fourth-grade teacher with initially sparking her interest in creative writing. She was determined at an early age to have her work published. When she was in the eighth grade she wrote a children's book and convinced her school yearbook publisher to put it in print.

Karen was born and raised in Dallas but now lives in Kansas City, Missouri. She has worked as a magazine art director, a free-lance writer and a textbook editor, but now she keeps herself busy full-time writing about romance.

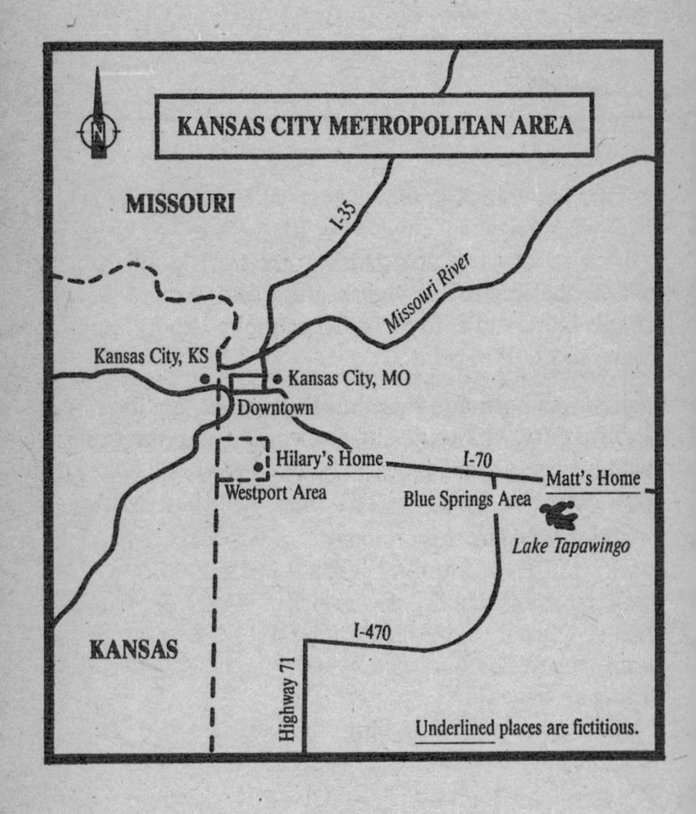
KANSAS CITY METROPOLITAN AREA
N
MISSOURI
I-35
Missouri River
Kansas City, KS
Kansas City, MO
Downtown
Hilary's Home
I-70
Matt's Home
Westport Area
Blue Springs Area
Lake Tapawingo
I-470
KANSAS
Highway 71
Underlined places are fictitious.

Chapter One

Hilary McShane shivered as she stood on the porch of her old frame house, her back to the front door. She watched with a growing sense of desolation as the tail-lights of the taxi receded into the unseasonably cool, misty night.

"Home again, home again," she murmured in the darkness, wishing now that she'd called Sheila to come pick her up at the airport instead of taking the cab. She hadn't wanted to drag her friend out of bed at this late hour, but if she had, she wouldn't be facing this dark house alone.

She fought off a coughing fit as she searched through her overflowing leather bag for her keys. At least her fever was down, Hilary thought as her fingers closed around the familiar shape of the wooden key chain. But her cough persisted. She fitted the key into the dead-bolt lock and, knowing from many past battles that the lock was stubborn, she gave it a healthy twist.

The key broke off in her hand.

Hilary stared at the twisted scrap of metal in dismay, silently cursing the spate of bad luck that seemed to be following her. She had hoped to creep into the house without awakening her house sitter, Meredith, but now she had no choice. She drew her hand into a fist and pounded on the wooden door. A few flakes of pink paint drifted down.

"Meredith?" she called out, and pounded again. There was no answer. After repeating the process, Hilary was forced to accept the fact that her house sitter wasn't in. Sheila had warned Hilary that her social-butterfly daughter often stayed out late. At the time Hilary hadn't minded, just so someone would be around to water the plants, collect the mail and give the house a lived-in look. Now she minded.

She'd spent almost twenty-four hours in transit from the wild Alaskan coast to Kansas City, counting layovers. All she'd thought about during that time was the warm bed that awaited her. She was too tired and too miserable to stand out here in the drizzle.

"Dammit," she muttered, "I'm getting into this house one way or another." She left her purse and duffel bag on the porch. Stepping gingerly through the wet grass, she carefully made her way around to the side of her house until she stood under the dormer that sheltered her second-story bedroom window. She knew the lock on that window was broken. A large twisted oak tree towered over the roof, with one branch stretching conveniently close to the window.

As a child, Hilary had scampered up and down this tree with the agility of a monkey. Could she still do it? With a resigned sigh she set about scaling the rough trunk.

The climb wasn't as easy as she remembered, especially when she was tired and a bit weak from her illness, and the tree bark was slick with rain. But after several miserable minutes of slow, unsteady progress, she made it high enough that she could scoot out onto the branch, then swing her legs down until her toes touched the relative safety of the windowsill. Hilary would have smiled at her own success if it wasn't such an effort.

The window protested with a shriek of wood against wood, but the warmth inside the house beckoned her. She stuck one leg through the opening and promptly upset a lamp, which tumbled noisily to the floor. She was about to push on through the opening anyway when she heard a strange sound. She froze, her heart pounding. Someone was in her bedroom. Though it was dark and quiet, she knew with an unshakable certainty that she was not alone.

"Meredith?" she whispered hopefully.

A low, deadly-sounding and very male voice answered her. "Hold it right there."

She willed on herself a calmness she didn't feel. She'd interrupted a burglar! "Look, I'll just back on out of here, okay?"

"What the hell?" The voice was filled with irritation and confusion. Through the darkness Hilary saw the shadow of movement near the lamp on the floor. With a click, the room was illuminated, and suddenly standing before her was six feet of half-dressed man brandishing her high school softball trophy like an avenging broadsword.

"You're a woman," he said, slowly lowering the trophy.

Hilary was only too aware of that fact. The pleasingly sculpted man standing before her in blue bikini briefs sharpened her tired senses, including an overwhelming sense of her own femininity that was disconcerting under the circumstances.

"I'm the woman who owns this house," she corrected him, pulling her other leg through the window.

"Wouldn't the front door have been simpler?"

"Never mind about me. Who are you? And where's Meredith?" She glanced over at the rumpled sheets. "What are you doing sleeping in my bed?" Inwardly she groaned. She'd wanted to sound intimidating, and instead she'd come off like Goldilocks.

"I'm Matthew Burke, Meredith's cousin." He smiled slowly. "And you're Hilary McShane. Now I recognize you from your picture." He nodded toward a framed photograph on the wall, which featured Hilary with her grandmother. She'd been perhaps twenty-four when the photo was taken, but she hadn't changed much in the few years since.

The muscles around Matthew's neck and shoulders visibly untensed as he assumed a more relaxed posture. "Didn't Aunt Sheila write to tell you I was staying here?" he asked.

Now things were beginning to make sense, Hilary thought. "She probably did. The MammalTrackers project was so far out in the boonies we hadn't received any mail—" She stopped to accommodate another coughing fit.

"You sound awful." He tossed the forgotten trophy onto the bed. "You'll catch pneumonia in those wet clothes." He reached to help her remove her sodden jacket. She let him, then was surprised at how sure and gentle his hands felt where they brushed against her sweater.

"Too late," she said. "I already have pneumonia. That's why I'm home a couple of months early. So, Matthew—"

"Matt," he corrected her.

"Matt," she repeated. "Why are you here instead of Meredith?"

"Meredith injured her knee a couple of weeks ago playing volleyball, and she had to move back home with Aunt Sheila. But Sheila didn't want to leave your house empty. It just so happened I needed a place to stay..." He shrugged as he hung her jacket on the corner of the four-poster bed. "Would you excuse me a moment?" He opened the top drawer of the oak chest and produced a pair of jeans.

Hilary couldn't compel herself to look away as he dressed. He was about her own age, she guessed. His brown hair was thick and almost straight, and it fell over his forehead as he bent over to step into the jeans. His body was lean but firm, his actions graceful yet economical. She was fascinated with the way his softly faded jeans molded to his lean hips and thighs.

When he looked up at her again, she was struck by his eyes. It wasn't the deep brown color so much as the way they seemed to take in every detail of her bedraggled appearance. Her heartbeat stumbled.

"Are you ready?" he asked.

Had she missed something? "Ready for what?"

"A hot bath. Your teeth are chattering."

Hilary longed to argue. Why should she take the advice of this man? But the fact of the matter was that she was too tired to argue, and the prospect of a steamy soak in the tub was heavenly. She *was* shivering. So she followed meekly as Matt took her arm and led her out of the bedroom and down the hall.

They paused at the bathroom door.

"You look pale," he commented, a note of concern in his voice. "Can you manage the bath on your own?"

"Of course I can manag-g-ge." Her chattering teeth betrayed her.

Matt's brows drew together as he reached a hand up to her forehead. "You feel warm. Are you taking any kind of medicine?"

"I'm fine," she said a bit sharply, shying away from a touch that felt too familiar, too comforting—too intimate—to have come from a stranger. But even as she pulled back, she realized she was only fighting herself. Matthew Burke was going to take care of her, and there wasn't anything she could do about it.

She attempted to soften her retort with a smile. "I have some antibiotics in my purse, and I'm due for one. If you could bring my things up from the front porch, I'd appreciate it."

He didn't smile back as concern continued to etch his face. "Be careful getting in the tub. You're pretty shaky."

She was, Hilary admitted as she leaned against the bathtub to turn on the faucet. But she wasn't sure she needed or wanted Matt's concern. She'd gotten enough of that from the doctor in Alaska to last a lifetime. She'd been sent home under protest, insisting she was hardly sick at all.

Downstairs, Matt found one damp duffel bag and one overstuffed leather purse on the front porch. This was all she took with her on a three-month camping trip in Alaska? Definitely the adventuresome type, he decided.

He'd deduced a great deal about Hilary McShane long before tonight. He knew she was unconventional, partly due to hints his aunt had dropped about her neighbor, but mostly because of what he'd seen of Hilary's house.

The walls were painted in bright, offbeat colors, and the furnishings, from antique to ultramodern, were eclectic—and that was a kind description. Every surface in the house was loaded with knickknacks and bric-a-brac, from framed photos to jars filled with matchbooks to dozens of souvenir teacups from all over the country. The paintings and photos she'd chosen to hang on the walls were mismatched except with respect to their subject matter; they were exclusively devoted to wildlife.

Then there was the outside of the house. It was painted pink. Matt had always wanted to know what kind of person lived in a pink house. Now he knew—or at least, he'd found out enough that he wanted to know more.

She'd started to get under his skin the moment he'd turned on that lamp and seen her long legs straddling the windowsill. Her mop of coppery hair was damp from the mist and curling in wild disarray. He'd immediately liked the determined thrust of her chin and her slightly raspy voice, surprisingly low and sultry, which had played against his nerves like a good back scratch. Thank God his jeans had been handy.

Still, he would have liked to have met her under different circumstances. Now that she was here, it was only a matter of minutes before she'd attempt to oust him from her home.

He couldn't afford to be evicted. Over the past two weeks he had filled the greenhouse out back with plantings. To move his seedlings now would defeat the whole purpose of his summer research project. Yet what choice did the woman have but to reclaim her home?

Upstairs again, he listened at the bathroom door. Upon hearing a definite splashing noise, he nodded with satisfaction and knocked. "Hilary?"

"You can come in. I have the curtain drawn."

Too bad, he caught himself thinking as he opened the door cautiously. "I brought your things. I'd like to find the antibiotics for you, but I don't dare put my hand in this bag of yours. God knows what I might run into."

From behind the curtain she gave a low chuckle. Matt felt it move through him like a warm breeze. "Just dump everything on the floor," she suggested, apparently unconcerned at the state of her purse. "Look for a brown bottle."

Matt stared into the bag dubiously. "Okay, if you say so." He tipped it over, then watched in fascination as a small avalanche of Hilary's personal belongings spilled and formed a mountain on the floor. A wallet, a glasses case, a checkbook, several lipsticks, a nail file, a package of tissues, a granola bar, a Swiss Army knife, a pair of *socks*? A roll of stamps, three postcards. Would it never *end*? Finally a tall, slim bottle of the sought-after prescription medicine rolled out.

"It sounds like you just unloaded a dump truck full of tire jacks onto the bathroom floor," Hilary commented.

"It looks worse than that." Matt filled a paper cup from the tap and handed it to her around the edge of the curtain, along with one of the red-and-yellow capsules. He resisted the urge to inch the curtain back just a tiny bit.

"Thanks. I'm really not all that sick, you know. It's a very mild case of pneumonia. I've been taking these horse pills for a couple of days, and I'm definitely on the mend. But that irritating doctor still wouldn't let me—" she coughed "—stay on."

"You were whale-watching, right? With that cough you might have scared the whales all the way back to Hawaii," Matt said as he began to scoop the mountain of things back into her purse.

How could anyone stand to be this disorganized? he wondered. But then he'd already known that about her just from the state of her kitchen. Everything was spotless—he couldn't fault her housekeeping. But how could she stand to work in there? The forks were mixed in with the spoons. The pasta was on the same shelf as the peanut butter. It made him cringe just thinking about it.

On the other hand, thinking about the woman herself caused a reaction of a completely different nature.

"The MammalTrackers doctor said the cold, wet weather in Alaska wouldn't do the pneumonia any good," she continued, oblivious to his less-than-pure thoughts. "But conditions aren't much better here."

"The weather's supposed to dry up and turn warm tomorrow," he answered automatically as he tried, unsuccessfully, to banish the persistent mental image he had of her nude figure reclining in the tub. He knew he had to get out of there. He had no business hanging around a strange woman's bath, anyway.

"How about I make us some tea?" he asked, rising to leave. "Unless you'd rather we just went right to bed."

"Really, Mr. Burke." She laughed easily.

"I meant by our respective selves, of course." Freudian slip? he wondered. He seldom made gaffes like that.

"No, I'm sure I couldn't sleep until we've discussed our little predicament," she said. "I'll join you downstairs shortly."

He heard water gurgling down the drain as he closed the bathroom door behind him and headed downstairs. At least she was open to discussion about their living arrangements, he thought, filling the copper teakettle from a bottle of distilled water. Maybe she wouldn't throw him out right away. Maybe she wouldn't throw him out at all. That was an intriguing thought.

Upstairs, Hilary wrapped a towel around her wet body. The terry cloth felt rough against her breasts. She glanced at herself in the mirror, deciding she didn't look pale at all, but decidedly flushed. Was it her medication? Or was it Matt?

She'd done a fair job of keeping up a neutral conversation when she was in the tub, but all the while she'd been acutely aware of him. When he'd given her the medicine, his hand had briefly, innocently, touched hers. She'd immediately developed a case of head-to-toe goose bumps.

Such a reaction wasn't normal, not for her. She'd shared very close quarters with the MammalTrackers team. Consequently she'd seen at least half a dozen men in their underwear over the past couple of weeks. Some of them were undoubtedly good-looking, yet none of them had caused her body to flare with awareness. Why Matt?

She tiptoed to the bedroom and opened the closet. Her clothes had been pushed to the very back, she noticed, to make room for Matt's things: long-sleeved and short-sleeved shirts, a half dozen of each, neatly categorized; three pairs of pants, precisely creased. The coat hangers were all evenly spaced, as if someone had taken a ruler to them.

Her old flannel wrapper was nowhere to be found. But his comfortable-looking blue terry robe hung on the door, invitingly convenient. Impulsively she plucked it off the hook and slipped into its warm, soft folds, wrapping her arms about herself briefly before tying the belt.

The faint noises coming from the kitchen downstairs reminded Hilary that she had an appointment for tea. She'd have to tell Matt immediately, of course, that he needed to find a new place to live. Determined to be firm, she made her way downstairs. But all her determination was forgotten as Hilary got a good look at her kitchen.

It was her kitchen, wasn't it?

Her normally jumbled and tarnished pots and pans, which she'd hung haphazardly from a rack over the stove, now sported a like-new shine and were hung from largest to smallest, left to right. Her copper canisters, which she usually stashed here and there all about the kitchen, were arranged neatly on one countertop—largest to smallest, left to right. Other than a knife rack, the counters were devoid of any other items—no cereal boxes or stray coffee cups, no popcorn popper, no toaster. The refrigerator door, which always featured a collage of drawings and paintings by her students, was bare except for an orderly procession of magnets lined up like little soldiers.

Hilary was afraid to touch anything, afraid of disturbing the rigid order. And oddly enough, the man standing at the stove making tea looked completely at home. He'd put on a T-shirt, she noted with relief. She didn't need to be distracted by that broad expanse of bare chest.

"Why did you do this to my kitchen?" she asked cautiously.

Matt whirled around. "Oh, there you are. I just straightened up a little...." He paused, eyeing her curiously. She wondered if she'd been too presumptuous in borrowing his robe, after all. "You'll find it much more efficient than it was before," he continued, looking away. "Do you want citrus or raspberry tea?"

"Raspberry. No, citrus. I mean, it doesn't matter. What happened to all the stuff on my fridge?"

"It's all safe. Don't worry," he said, setting two cups of tea down on the table. "I didn't want anything to happen to it while you were away. Here." He opened one of the small overhead cabinets, the ones she never used because she couldn't reach them without standing on a chair. She noticed they were full of plastic storage containers now. Matt pulled down a manila folder and handed it to her. The folder was labeled: Hilary McShane's Refrigerator Artwork. How precise. Inside were all of her students' pictures.

Without a word, Hilary began returning the pictures to their rightful places on the refrigerator. "My students visit me sometimes. It's important they see how much I value their work."

"I see. I'm sorry. I shouldn't have bothered the pictures."

Hilary felt suddenly contrite herself, for getting her feathers ruffled over such a trifling matter. It was just that she wasn't used to anyone disturbing her things.

"I didn't mean to snap," she said after a few moments. "It's late, I'm tired, and I wasn't ready for the surprise of finding a strange man in my house."

Matt joined her at the small kitchen table. He blew on his tea to cool it. "Coming through the window as you did, you were a bit of a surprise yourself." He laughed, and the sound of it dissolved her irritation. "At first I thought you were a burglar."

"That's what I thought about you, till I realized a burglar wouldn't be running around in his underwear."

"Yes. Well." He cleared his throat and took a sip of tea.

Hilary became suddenly aware of the deep V at the front of the robe. She pulled the right lapel more tightly over the left. "Anyhow, now that we both know who the other is, that brings us to the real problem. You can make other living arrangements, I presume."

"Tonight?" Matt's eyebrows shot up.

"No, of course not. I'm not unreasonable. But I'm sure you can find some other place to live by the end of the week."

The end of the week. That gave Matt four days in which to convince her he had to stay. "Is there a chance you'll be returning to Alaska when you've recovered?" he asked hopefully.

"Don't I wish. Unfortunately the project has a waiting list of volunteers. My replacement is already on the way. Anyway, I can't afford another round-trip ticket to Alaska, not on a teacher's salary." She took a long sip of her tea. "I'm afraid my whale-watching days are over."

At that moment Matt really did feel for her. It was a tough break, her getting sick and having to give up her vacation, though he'd never heard of a less appealing vacation. He couldn't imagine that anyone would want to pay money to spend the summer freezing in Alaska, bumping around in a little boat looking for whales. But she must have enjoyed it, or she wouldn't look so wistful right now.

He studied her for a moment, intrigued by the combination of fragility and toughness she represented. As her hair dried, it curled into red-gold tendrils that framed her delicate face. Her eyes were big, with smoky green irises that seduced even as they snapped with anger, as they had a few moments ago. Her mouth was full and generous, her teeth white and straight. But her tongue could be sharp.

"Sheila mentioned you were a teacher," he said in an attempt to distract her from her thoughts. "What do you teach?"

She brightened immediately. "Art. Couldn't you guess?" she answered, nodding toward the refrigerator at the gallery she'd just rehung. "I teach in the gifted program, third grade through junior high at several different schools. It's simply amazing what some kids can accomplish if you just give them the incentive to unleash their artistic talents. See that picture of the dog?" She pointed to a surrealistic watercolor painting on the refrigerator.

He couldn't necessarily identify the animal in the painting as anything remotely canine, but it did have a definite hangdog expression. "He looks sad," Matt commented.

"Look at the title of the painting, at the bottom."

He read it aloud. "'A Trip to the Vet.' Hey, that is cute. How old is this little Picasso?"

"As a matter of fact, your own cousin Bryan did that a couple of years ago. He was only eight at the time. He's a mathematics whiz, you know, and already his teachers are pushing him to be a computer programmer or some such nonsense. Thank goodness Sheila encourages his creativity."

"Computers can be a creative field," Matt countered. "So can science."

Hilary disagreed. "Science has always struck me as dull, maddeningly precise and methodical. Even when I was working with MammalTrackers, I just wanted to see the humpbacks and listen to their songs. The statistics and the high-tech equipment bored me."

"Really? And yet you still enjoyed participating?"

She nodded enthusiastically. "It got to be a standing joke. I was so bad at recording data that they took my pencil away from me. Most days I was relegated to driving the boat, which was more my style anyway. Scientific methodology has a way of getting on my nerves."

She paused to sip her tea. "So, anyway, what do you do, Matt?"

"I'm a horticulturist."

"Oh. That's a sort of scientist, isn't it?" Hilary's translucent skin showed her blush to perfection. But immediately she brightened again, easily overcoming her embarrassment. "Sure, Sheila's told me about you. The plant guy from Blue Springs, right?"

He nodded, not positive he liked having his entire identity as a researcher summed up as "the plant guy." "I develop and test hybrid varieties of flowers and vegetables," he clarified.

"So you grow flowers with bigger blossoms, and plants that yield more vegetables, is that it?"

"That's about the gist of it. In fact, even as we speak, your greenhouse is just overflowing with seedlings I plan to work with during the summer. Which brings us to a sticky problem."

Hilary pursed her lips. "You can't just pick up and move out tomorrow," she concluded.

"Exactly. I'm having my own house and greenhouse remodeled. I'd planned to take a break from the plants and do some reading and studying this summer. Then Sheila told me about your place, with this huge, empty greenhouse, and I couldn't resist moving in and taking on a job for a seed company."

"You can't just move the plants somewhere else?" Hilary asked.

Matt shrugged. "No place to move them to."

"Well, if it's just the greenhouse you're worried about, you're welcome to it as long as you like. I didn't have any plans to use it this summer—what's wrong?"

"I appreciate your generosity, but that doesn't really solve my problem. You see, I also have a lot of seedlings in the basement, under the grow lights."

"Then you can have free run of the basement, too," Hilary suggested. "That's no problem. There's an outside entrance, so you won't bother me."

"Then there's the matter of the den..."

"You mean my art studio?"

"Well, it *was* your studio. I moved some of your things out—"

"You what?" Her voice rose several decibels.

"Just temporarily. I needed room for my books and my computer and my files. I had every intention of returning your things to just the way I found them, and I still will, of course, but—"

She set her teacup down with a thud and pushed her chair back from the table. "What else have you taken over?" she asked through tightly clenched teeth. "You'd better lay it all out now."

He wished she wouldn't stare at him like that. Those smoky green eyes of hers did strange things to his nervous system. "I, um, that is..."

"Out with it!"

"I relocated a few rosebushes in the back. I needed that shady spot against that one wall for a small test garden—"

"You *moved* Grandma's rosebushes?" She stood, stiff-shouldered and straight-backed. "They've been growing there since before I was born!"

Matt couldn't quite grasp Hilary's violent objection to this last of his offenses. "I didn't hurt them. They're in a sunny spot by the garage, and as soon as I'm done here, I'll put them back where they—"

"Consider yourself done!" Hilary folded her arms across her chest, as if to ward off his next argument. "I want you and your things out of here tomorrow." She turned and started to leave.

"Hilary, wait!"

She ignored him, muttering under her breath as she hit the swinging door of the kitchen. "Those poor, poor roses. Poor things."

Matt followed her, grabbed her elbow, swung her around. "What did you say?"

"I said, 'Poor roses.' Now I'll never get them to bloom."

"Why do you say that?"

"Those were Grandma's favorite roses. She used to fuss over those bushes—I mean, she loved them, really loved them. And they loved her back by covering themselves with these huge, delicate pink blossoms. But after she died—" She paused and took a deep breath.

"What happened after she died?" he asked gently, immediately forgiving her for her fit of temper. She was obviously exhausted on top of being ill, and he'd done something to upset her. He wanted to understand what it was.

"They don't bloom anymore. For three years I've tried everything. I watered them, I fed them, I kept the aphids off. I talked to them, I sang to them—I even brought a tape recorder into the backyard and played Mozart for them. But I couldn't get a single bud."

"Maybe you're not feeding them the right thing," Matt offered. "Sometimes the slightest variation in soil or—"

She shook her head in an emphatic denial. "Grandma showed me how to take care of them. I do it exactly the same as she did. Don't you see? They're sad because she's gone. They need to be surrounded by love in order to bloom. And now you've gone and jerked them up out of their homes—"

"I did *not* jerk them up. I transplanted them with a great deal of care so as not to disturb their roots. And plants don't recognize emotions."

"How do you know?"

"Because if plants could think or feel, someone would have proved it by now. Enough people have tried."

"I take it you can't believe something without hard evidence, then," Hilary said, recovering her composure.

"That's right. I don't believe in UFOs, Loch Ness Monsters, psychic healing or things that go bump in the night."

"Then you obviously have no sense of imagination."

He didn't refute her criticism. "Look, Hilary, let's negotiate. What if I restrict myself to the greenhouse and the basement. You thought that was all right earlier."

She wavered, acknowledging that she might have let her temper override her common sense. As awful as she felt, she wasn't thinking too clearly—or acting too sensibly. "I'll have to think about it."

"You won't even know I'm here," he persisted. "And I'll pay you rent. Before you know it, you'll have enough money saved to go on another whale vacation."

That gave her pause. She never had enough money to finance her various environmental concerns. Still, she refused to make any snap decisions. "I told you, I'll think about it." Again she started to turn away from him toward the stairs.

"Oh, Hilary, one more thing. If you force me to relocate my seedlings, many of them will die. Do you want that on your conscience?"

She thought she saw him wink—or maybe it was her bleary eyes playing tricks on her.

"I'll just sack out on the couch for the rest of tonight," he said, turning toward the den. "You can tell me your decision in the morning."

As tired as she was, Hilary couldn't sleep. For one thing, her bed held *his* scent, an intoxicating blend of mysterious, unidentifiable but very male fragrances that preyed on her vulnerable imagination. But what really kept her awake was the way Matt had turned her own philosophy against her—a philosophy he had ridiculed.

And it was *working*. She wanted to be rid of the infuriating man, to sweep him out of her house and clutter everything up again so it felt like home. Still, all she could think about were his defenseless seedlings, crying out, "Save me, save me! Don't let me die!"

She knew it was ridiculous. But no amount of logic would force the disturbing image from her mind. She cursed her own gullibility. No wonder she was on the mailing list of every environmentalist organization in the country. She'd *saved* everything from baby seals to bees to prairie grass. Now she supposed it was up to her to save a greenhouse full of plants she'd never met, or suffer their deaths on her conscience. She didn't even know what kind of plants they were.

The sky was already beginning to gray with the approaching dawn when Hilary finally fell asleep. But even in her sleep she thrashed about until the bedcovers swirled around her like a cocoon. So she was almost grateful when a tentative knock on her door woke her up a couple of hours later.

"Hilary? You awake?"

"I am now." She began to cough.

Matt took that as his signal to enter. "I brought you some breakfast. And I picked up a bottle of cough medicine at the drugstore."

"Oh. That was...nice of you, but you really didn't have to."

"It was no trouble."

She did her best to straighten the covers, realizing after a moment's struggle that her nightshirt was bunching up around her hips. If she leaned forward once more, Matt was going to get an eyeful of bare pink skin. She stilled and drew the covers up to her ribs, smoothing a place where he could set down the breakfast tray.

"Eggs Benedict?" she asked hopefully, glancing at the plate on the tray.

"And freshly squeezed orange juice. But first this." He handed her the cough medicine and a large spoon.

She grimaced as she swallowed a mouthful of the bitter red liquid under his watchful eye. "This stuff is awful," she said, wiping tears from her eyes. "Tastes like battery acid."

"The worse it tastes, the better it works. At least, that's what my mother used to tell me."

"My mother told me that, too, but I still don't believe it. And if you think all this solicitude is going to influence my decision, you're wrong."

"I didn't think it could hurt," he countered. One corner of his mouth lifted slightly.

At least he was honest. She took an experimental bite of the egg concoction. It was heavenly. She scooted herself into a more upright position and placed the tray over her lap so that she could attack the food in earnest. "This is great. Where'd you learn to cook like this?"

"I was motivated by survival instinct. I live alone, I don't like restaurants, and I hate frozen dinners even more. But I love good food. So I bought a cookbook. I never found it difficult to follow a recipe."

"It must be the scientist in you. I love to cook—in fact, I'm a good cook. But I've learned most everything I know by watching my grandmother and through my own trial and error. I can't follow a recipe to save my life."

His dark eyes appraised her anew, twinkling with humor this time. She shivered, though the sun was shining brightly through the window and spilling onto her bed in big warm patches.

"When you finish with that," he said, "come downstairs. I have something to show you." He gave her a mysterious parting smile over his shoulder as he left.

Hilary didn't want to get dressed or venture downstairs. In fact, she'd just as soon lie in bed all day and get some much-needed rest. But all the same, she knew she'd answer Matt's summons, if for no other reason than because he'd piqued her curiosity. What did he have to show her?

And what was he so all-fired cheerful for, anyway? He had to suspect she was planning to evict him. She took another bite of the eggs Benedict and sighed delightedly, all negative thoughts banished. Maybe she'd let him stay.

When Hilary came downstairs a few minutes later, Matt caught himself staring at her, cataloging her assets once again. Her faded jeans emphasized the leanness of her legs, and the soft green sweater she wore heightened her dramatic coloring. What was it about her that intrigued him so? How could a disorganized schoolteacher, an eccentric one at that, make him feel so... aware?

"You have some color in your cheeks this morning," he commented, though he thought the bland compliment did her a disservice.

"No more buttering up, Matt," she grumbled, unable to mask the slight hint of appreciation in her voice. "Now what is this thing you want to show me?"

"It's outside." When she reached the bottom of the stairs, he took her hand and led her through the living room and out the sliding glass door.

"I don't want to look at your miserable little hybrid seedlings," she said, though she didn't resist as he led her across the small patio. His hand was surprisingly warm and comfortable around hers, as if they held hands every day. "If I'm going to evict them, I don't want to know them personally."

They passed the place where the rosebushes used to be. There was nothing there now but bare black dirt. Hilary deliberately looked the other way. They walked all the way to the detached garage.

"I got to feeling guilty about moving the roses, after all," Matt explained. "I didn't know you were sentimentally attached to them. Anyway, I couldn't sleep, and I came out here to check on them, make sure they weren't wilting or anything, and I found this."

They'd stopped in front of the transplanted rosebushes, which were now growing against a trellis next to the garage. "You've trimmed them back," Hilary accused.

"They'll grow. But look here." He pointed to a branch on one of the bushes.

Hilary leaned closer and squinted until at last she saw it. A tiny pale pink bud was just beginning to open itself to the morning sun.

Chapter Two

"That's amazing . . . unbelievable," Hilary murmured as she leaned down even closer to study the delicate bud. She did her best to ignore Matt's haughty smirk.

"What do you think of your 'poor, poor roses' now?" he asked.

"I don't know what to think." She examined each of the four bushes. They were short but healthy looking, with not a sign of a brown leaf or a garden pest. Apparently Matt hadn't hurt them after all. But did he have to be so smug?

"I suspect the bushes weren't getting enough sun," he explained. "See that redbud tree?" He lightly touched her shoulder to get her attention, then pointed to the tall tree standing near the corner of the house. "It's probably grown several feet in the past few years, enough to put too much shade on the roses."

His hand remained on her shoulder, muddling her thought processes. She had to take a reflexive half step away from him before she could respond. "Maybe the tree *has* grown, but the bushes stopped blooming abruptly, the very week my grandmother died. How do you explain that? The redbud didn't shoot up overnight."

"Maybe something foreign got into the soil. An excess of—"

"Oh, don't be so logical," she snapped, though she ruined the effect with a grin as she turned to look at the bloom again. She couldn't continue scowling when that little rosebud was growing so triumphantly.

"If it's not the soil, what's your explanation for that bloom?" Matt asked, crossing his muscular arms over his chest and staring at her with an oh-so-superior lift of one eyebrow.

"Obviously this bush likes you," Hilary stated matter-of-factly. "Although I can't figure out what it sees in you that I've missed."

Matt chose to ignore the dig. "Interesting theory. The roses didn't bloom for you—does that mean they don't like you?"

Hilary scowled again. "I don't know. Maybe they feel I'm not sincere. I take good care of them, and I want them to bloom, but I couldn't possibly love them the way Grandma did."

"And you think I do?" He rocked back on his heels and rolled his eyes skyward. "I assure you I have no emotional ties to any plants."

"But you were concerned. You came out here because you thought they might be wilting. Maybe they recognize a caring soul, even if you won't admit you are one. Plants react to emotions."

Matt laughed, a sound Hilary found unaccountably pleasing given the fact that they were in the middle of an argument. "That's utter nonsense," he said. "I gave them more sunlight, I got a bloom. Period. As you can see, I haven't hurt them. I was hoping that might convince you to let me stay."

Hilary glanced at the rose, then back at Matt. "Do you think the bushes will continue to bloom?"

He put a finger to his chin, seeming to give her question serious thought. "That depends on whether there's someone around to make them *want* to bloom."

He was using her own philosophy against her again. She sighed, defeated by the teasing glint she saw in Matt's dark eyes. "All right, I'll make a deal with you. You can have the greenhouse and the basement if you'll take care of the rosebushes. As long as they keep blooming, you can stay."

"What about the den?"

"Don't push your luck, pal. I need my studio space back."

He nodded resignedly. "Just thought I'd ask one more time."

"There's a spare bedroom upstairs," she heard herself saying. "It's not very big, but you can use it if you like."

He flashed her an easy smile, as if he'd known all along he'd get what he wanted. "Thanks, that's very generous—"

"Don't thank me, thank the roses," she quipped. "You're in their hands now. Oh, and one more thing. Don't reorganize anything else, okay? I appreciate the fact that you unpacked my cosmetic bag and put all my toiletries away, but did you have to line everything up according to size? When I opened the medicine cabinet, I thought I was in the Twilight Zone."

"I'll try not to, if it bothers you that much," he said, seemingly baffled by her attitude. "But you'd better not look at your houseplants till you're in a really good mood."

Cripes, what had he done to her plants? Ignoring his warning, Hilary immediately turned and started across the yard toward the patio door. She advanced at a military clip through the living room and into the glassed-in sun porch. Matt was right behind her.

She skidded to a halt at the sun porch doorway. Her happy tangle of greenery was gone. Not only had Matt trimmed the plants, he'd arranged them into a symmetrical pattern. He'd also untangled her English ivy. The runners were now stretched out along the sill of the bay window.

"What was wrong with how they looked before?" Her lips pursed into a thin, straight line.

"Nothing, but I wasn't aiming for aesthetics," he explained. "I put the varieties that need more light nearest the window, and the others farther back."

In lieu of a response to his maddeningly irrefutable logic, Hilary launched into a coughing fit. The man was certifiably compulsive.

"Do you need some water?" he asked, all concern once again.

She shook her head and cleared her throat one last time. "What I need is to get away from all this neatness. I'm going to visit my mother," she announced brusquely. "While I'm gone, would you put my studio back together?" It was a demand rather than a question. She whooshed out of the room without waiting for his response.

A few seconds later Matt heard the front door slam. Shaking his head, he retreated to the greenhouse to water the seedlings, refusing to admit that Hilary's harsh words rankled him. He hoped she'd mellow out after she got to feeling better. He didn't relish the thought of tiptoeing around her for the rest of the summer.

Neither would he consciously admit that her rare smiles reached right to the pit of his stomach, or that her soft red-gold hair made his fingers itch to touch it. He squashed those disturbing images before they fully formed.

Instead he took comfort from the orderliness of his plantings, the trays filled with neat rows of small square pots. The precision demanded in the scientific world had always pleased him. The sight of his work in progress tended to reaffirm that all was right with the world.

He'd never doubted what direction his life would take, and he'd never once regretted the path he'd selected. He derived tremendous enjoyment from pressing a seed into rich, fertile soil and watching it sprout and develop. He found it even more exciting to discover the factors that influenced that growth.

He pulled a tape measure from his pocket and randomly measured some of the seedlings, recording his results on clipboards. The tomatoes were progressing exactly according to his projections.

It was too soon to tell much about his latest crop of hybrid roses, however. The tiny green sprouts were just beginning to break the surface of the growing medium, and it would be a couple of months before any blooms would appear. He made one final check of everything before returning to the house.

Matt decided to take advantage of Hilary's absence and move his things into the spare bedroom. It would be easier to transfer his belongings, he reasoned, when he wasn't tripping over her around every corner.

First he lugged his computer and several armloads of books upstairs into the small cubicle. He cast a jaundiced eye at the twin bed, knowing it wouldn't give him a good night's sleep without a fight. Next he retrieved Hilary's painting supplies from the closet where he'd stored them. He set up the easel and paints in the den just as he'd first found them, curbing his urge to reorganize. At this point he didn't want to step on her toes and threaten her generosity.

He hadn't looked closely at her canvases before, but now he did. One of the paintings still in progress featured a table littered with the remains of what looked like Sunday breakfast for two, including a rumpled newspaper open to the funnies. It was wonderfully realistic, a whimsical slice of life. It was also undeniably sensuous.

Each picture was equally evocative, almost overflowing with vivid, rich hues. Matt felt the urge to touch the canvases. He inhaled deeply and decided he liked the smell of paints and linseed oil. He didn't know much about art, but Hilary must be talented to elicit such a response in him.

Reluctantly Matt left the paintings and set about moving the rest of his things to the tiny bedroom. Other than the tools of his trade, he hadn't brought much with him from home, just some casual clothes and the usual toiletries. If he needed anything else, his home in Blue Springs was only a thirty-minute drive away.

He debated whether to move the TV and VCR upstairs. They were the only extravagances he'd brought from home. Actually Matt considered them more of a necessity. How else could he record the Royals' games?

In the end, he decided to leave the video setup where it was unless Hilary complained. The unit wouldn't fit in his new quarters, anyway.

He put off moving his clothing until last, feeling like a guilty trespasser as he entered the bedroom Hilary had reclaimed. The room was imbued with her presence now, her light, subtle fragrance—and her clutter. The clothes from her duffel bag were strewn about the room and the ivory bedsheets were wildly disheveled.

Reflexively he started to make the bed, then checked himself. He supposed Hilary's orders against reorganizing included picking up clothes and straightening linens.

She was a unique species of female, he mused, sinking onto the edge of the antique bed. He pulled her lace-edged pillow against him unconsciously as he pictured her in his mind. She was nothing like the no-nonsense women he usually socialized with. She was more alive, more vivid somehow, like big-screen Technicolor compared to black-and-white TV.

On the other hand, she had a quick temper. By all logic he should have disliked her, but he couldn't bring himself to. Perhaps that was because she had every right to be in a lousy mood, given her pneumonia. At any rate, her occasional prickliness was tempered by an undeniable vein of compassion. She was obviously soft on whales and roses—and perhaps a little soft in the head as well, though he had to admit he found her offbeat ways somewhat endearing.

When Matt realized he was pressing his face into her pillow, he forced himself to get a grip on reality. Such soul-stirring thoughts about Hilary McShane could only lead to pointless frustration, for there was virtually no chance of anything other than tolerance forming between them. They had about as much in common as a wildflower and a tree stump, he thought, casting himself as the stump, and if there was one thing he firmly believed about relationships, it was that two people had to have some things in common.

A noise at the front door brought him back to awareness. Had Hilary returned from her mother's already? Quickly he retrieved his clothing and went downstairs to investigate.

"Yoo-hoo, Matt, are you home?" a feminine voice called.

"Right here, Sheila, come on in." Matt took the remaining stairs two at a time. He met up with his aunt just inside the front door.

"What are you doing, moving out already?" Sheila teased when she saw the armload of clothes he carried.

"After a fashion. Pour yourself a cup of coffee. I'll be with you as soon as I put these away."

"Oh, Matt, give me those." She took the clothes away from him and dropped them into a chair in the entryway. "The clothes can wait. Is something wrong? I could have sworn I saw Hilary's car barreling past my place a few minutes ago, but I knew it couldn't be." She led the way into the kitchen, then gasped. "My God, Matt, what have you done to Hilary's kitchen?"

"That's odd. Hilary reacted the same way."

"Then she *is* home? Oh, dear." Sheila sank her short, pudgy frame onto one of the kitchen chairs. "She was supposed to be gone till late August. What happened?"

"She had to cut the trip short. She—"

"And she's throwing you out just like that?"

"No, not exactly, though it was a close call. We didn't exactly hit it off. She hadn't received your letter, so she was more than a little surprised to find me here. But we've worked everything out. We've agreed to cohabit."

Sheila's eyebrows shot up at that.

"But I imagine we'll be staying clear of each other," he added quickly.

She looked only slightly less disapproving as she drummed her fingers on the tabletop. "Why'd she come home early, anyway?"

"Pneumonia."

"Pneumonia?" Sheila's hand flew to her mouth. "Hilary's never sick."

"It's a mild case, just a bad cough at this point," Matt said, patting his aunt's hand reassuringly.

The worried frown didn't leave Sheila's round face. "Oh, the poor dear. Where is she now? I hope she's not too put out with me for inviting you here."

"She said she was going to visit her mother."

"Are you . . . sure you heard right?"

"That's what she said." He set a mug in front of Sheila and filled it with coffee.

"Matt," Sheila said, leaving the coffee untasted. "Hilary's mother has been dead for at least a dozen years."

"Really? Then I must have misunderstood." He tried to sound unconcerned, but the small misunderstanding bothered him. He had a sharp eye and a keen ear for detail, and he didn't like making mistakes.

"You don't suppose she's snapped, do you?" Sheila asked in a hushed voice. "Maybe her illness is worse than you think. Maybe she's delirious with fever, and she thinks her mother is still alive."

Matt dismissed that idea. "She has a bad cough, but I would have noticed if she were delirious." He tried to recall Hilary's exact words. "I could swear that she said she was going to visit her mother . . . a cemetery perhaps?"

Sheila smiled in agreement. "Sure, of course. Hilary told me her mom is buried in Saint Martin's Cemetery in

Westside. Oh, but why would she go there when she's sick?"

"My fault," Matt confessed. "She wouldn't have run off if I hadn't—dammit, she ought to be home in bed." He stood decisively. "The cemetery's only a few minutes from here, right?"

Sheila nodded uncertainly. "You aren't going to—"

"I'm just going to drive by, see if she's there, make sure she's okay. If she does have a fever, she might not be thinking too clearly."

"Want me to go with you?"

"Actually, you could do something else to help. Do you think you could mess up the kitchen?"

Sheila's expressive eyebrows rose again. "Beg your pardon?"

"You know, make it look like it did—" and he gave a small shudder "—before I cleaned it up. To keep the peace, I'd like to return things to the way they were, but I'm not sure I can bring myself to duplicate that...mess."

"Her kitchen wasn't a mess," Sheila argued. "It was what you'd call—busy. But I'll do my best to untidy things up, if that's what you want."

"Thanks, Sheila. I'll be back in a few minutes." He pecked her on the cheek before heading out.

Matt pondered his own motivations as he turned the ignition key and his car roared to life. Certainly Hilary was in no immediate danger of suffering from exposure. It was warm and sunny, with only the hint of a breeze. Why, then, did he feel this compulsion to follow her?

Was it because her angry exit didn't sit well with him? Was it because he couldn't stand to do nothing and just wait for her to return, not knowing whether she'd still be upset? What did it matter, anyway? He'd known her less than half a day. Why couldn't he just let her be?

* * *

Hilary glanced around the cemetery to make sure it was really deserted. But there wasn't a soul around—at least, not a living soul, she chuckled to herself. The tall trees and hedges shielded her from the street's view so she could do as she pleased unobserved.

She flopped onto the ground and stretched out on her back between her mother's and grandmother's grave markers. The sun had evaporated last night's rain, so the freshly mown grass rubbing against her back was warm and dry. It made her glad to be back in the Midwest—or, at least, not so dispirited. Whale-watching had been an exciting adventure, but Alaska could get damnably cold, even in the summer.

Unlike most people, Hilary liked cemeteries. This one made her feel especially comfortable, with its tall trees and well-tended shrubbery. Years ago her grandmother had taken her to this place on a regular basis so that she could continue to feel close to her mother. Hilary had always found those visits comforting. Even now, she still came here sometimes to talk to both her maternal relatives. She half believed they could hear her better when she communicated from this spot.

"Hi, Mama, Grandma, how are things in your part of the cosmos?" Hilary asked aloud as she stared up at the cloudless sky. "Bet they're better than things down here. I guess you must have figured out by now that I'm not in Alaska like I planned. I'm sick, but I'm getting better so there's no call to worry. My real problem is there's a man living in my house."

That certainly sounded scandalous, she mused.

"Now don't look so aghast." Hilary could easily envision the two women's shocked faces. In her imagination she clearly saw her mother with her deep red hair hanging thick and straight to her shoulders. And Hilary imagined her grandmother at her most robust and healthy, as she'd been before her illness.

"The man's a boarder, more or less, not a lover," Hilary went on to explain in her one-sided conversation. "But he's causing me more trouble than any lover I ever had...er, I mean any lover I could imagine.

"No, he's not an ogre or anything. In fact, he's quite good-looking...." What an understatement! "But we just can't get along. He rubs me...the wrong way." Her thoughts faltered as an image sprang into her mind unbidden, an image of Matt running firm, callused fingers along her spinal column, rubbing her the *right* way. She squeezed her eyes shut to dispel the intruding mental picture, fervently hoping her dear departed couldn't read everything in her mind.

"What am I going to do about Matthew Burke?" she asked, sitting up to stare at first one granite headstone, then the other. "I wish one of you would give me an answer. I can't seem to think. Matt spells trouble, I just know it, and yet... I'm almost glad I decided to let him stay. Does that make sense?"

No, of course not. The voice of Hilary's grandmother echoed in her mind. *Human emotions seldom make any sense.*

"What do you think, Mama? What should I do?"

Suddenly a phrase popped into Hilary's head, a favorite saying of her mother's: *When life hands you a lemon, make lemonade.* That was hardly the answer she'd wished for. What an eternal optimist her mother had been, Hilary mused. An uneducated woman trying to earn a decent living for herself and her child couldn't have had much to be cheerful about, and yet Iris

McShane had always seemed to be smiling, or singing, or whistling.

Hilary was like that herself, most of the time. "Why can't I just laugh this off, Mama? It's only for one summer. I can put up with him that long."

Put up with him? her alter-ego mother countered. *Make lemonade, Hilary my girl.*

Hilary sighed and fell back onto the grass, cushioning her head with her arms. With Matthew Burke around, she'd need a whole lot of sugar to make lemonade.

Once he found the cemetery, Matt had no trouble finding Hilary. That red-gold hair of hers reflected the sunlight like a beacon. He moved from tree to tree, making a zigzagging path toward her. All the while he told himself that he had no intention of intruding on a private moment. He just wanted to make sure she was all right.

When he got a little closer, he realized that she was lying down. *Lying down?* In a *cemetery*? He abandoned all pretense of stealth and sprinted straight for her. Her eyes appeared to be closed. Had she passed out?

"Hilary?" he said softly as he bent over her. He started to shake her, but the moment his hand touched her arm, her green eyes flew open and she bolted upright.

"What are you doing here?" she demanded in her most bristly voice.

He should have known to expect a chilly reception, but that didn't mean he had to like it. He had no ready reply to her question, so instead of answering, he settled onto the grass beside her and studied her porcelain profile.

She didn't return his gaze, but he had the distinct impression that she was fully aware of him, observing him in her peripheral vision.

"I was afraid you'd fainted," he finally said.

"Fainted? Whatever gave you that idea?"

"Most people don't lie down in a cemetery—unless they're one of the permanent residents."

"I was just relaxing. I happen to like this place. What are you doing here?" she repeated, a little less bristly this time. "How did you know where to find me, anyway?"

"Sheila and I figured it out. I was worried about you," he admitted. "You shouldn't be all alone out in the open with that terrible cough. I came to make sure you were all right." Without thinking he reached out to brush the dried grass from her back. Her sweater felt soft as a cloud against his palm. He ran his fingertips along first one shoulder blade, then the other.

Hilary expelled a long, deep breath. The sound, as hushed as it was, startled Matt. His gaze rose to meet hers. When he saw the astonishment in her eyes, he knew he'd overstepped his bounds. He drew back his hand and looked away.

"It's kind of you to be concerned," she said after a few moments, her voice more subdued now. "But I'm not an invalid. And even if I were, you shouldn't feel responsible for me."

"Apparently I drove you out of your own house. I can't help feeling responsible."

"Forget it," she said, dismissing his concern.

But he couldn't seem to forget or dismiss their disagreement. He refused to let her stay mad at him! He glanced at the nearby headstones, trying to make sense of his thoughts.

"Your mother?" he asked, gesturing toward the marker to their right, which bore Iris McShane's name.

Hilary nodded with a slight smile. "And the other one is Grandma. Eileen O'Keefe O'Leary. Have you ever heard such an Irish name? I inherited the famed temper from both sides of the family, I'm afraid." She hesitated a moment, then continued. "It was my own bad temper that drove me out of the house, not you." She absently picked a yellow dandelion and twirled it between her fingers.

She'd made an apology of sorts, so Matt took it as one. He might not get a better note on which to exit. Though he would have liked to enjoy the peacefulness of the cemetery with Hilary awhile longer, if he didn't put some distance between them, he'd reach out to touch her again. "I'll leave you alone now, if you're sure you're okay," he said as he stood up. "I didn't mean to intrude."

Hilary watched him stride away. From this perspective, his wide shoulders and lean hips formed a pleasing inverted triangle. The artist in her studied the shape of him, while the woman in her wondered why he made her shiver inside when she was warm on the outside. When she could no longer see him, she felt unaccountably lonely, filled with a sudden, overwhelming ache.

"Mama, Grandma, in case you were wondering, that's the guy," she murmured, though this time she sensed no answering words.

She remained a few minutes longer, but the relative peace she'd found earlier had deserted her. She waved goodbye to the headstones and headed back to her car.

When Hilary pulled up in the gravel driveway, she noticed for the first time the strange car parked at the curb. Pretty racy for a scientist, she mused. The silver-blue Saab wasn't new by any means, but Matt obviously kept it immaculate.

She glanced at the back seat of her ancient Chevy, known around the neighborhood as the Green Bomb. Empty paper bags from the nearby deli littered the floor.

She'd be willing to bet not so much as a gum wrapper or piece of lint marred the Saab's interior.

As she entered through the front door, she heard noises coming from the kitchen. Was he cleaning up again? The man was obsessed. But she unruffled herself when she found it was Sheila rummaging around in her cabinets.

Sheila spun around in surprise, then her face melted into a cliché of motherly concern. "Honey, are you all right?" she asked as she put a solicitous arm around Hilary's shoulders. "Matt told me you had pneumonia. You must feel just awful!"

"Not so bad, really." Hilary forced a smile for Sheila's benefit. "And speaking of Matt, you sure know how to pick a house sitter. Where is Mr. Clean, anyway?" She set her purse down on the kitchen table with a *clunk*, then sat herself down in a chair with only slightly more dignity.

"He's a darn sight more responsible than Meredith, I know that. Now come on, what do you *really* think of him?"

Hilary ignored the obvious twinkle in her friend's eye. "Matthew Burke ought to hire himself out as an efficiency expert. I've never seen anyone so compulsively neat."

"There are worse habits, you know," said Sheila. "You grew up in a household of women. You have no idea how messy men can be, what with leaving their socks all over the place—and those little beard stubbles in the sink! I wish my husband would take a lesson from Matt. Just think, the woman who marries him would probably never have to touch a vacuum cleaner again as long as she lives."

Sheila was right about one thing, Hilary thought. She'd never shared a house with a man, not even her father, and the sheer maleness of Matt's presence seemed even more pronounced in the very female environment of her grandmother's house. No man had lived here since her grandfather had died, shortly after her birth.

"Just the same, all that rigid order makes me jumpy," Hilary confessed. For the first time she noticed that her kitchen was decidedly *dis*orderly. "What were you doing in here, anyway?"

"Matt knew you didn't like the way he'd reorganized," Sheila explained, "and he wanted to put the kitchen back the way it was, but he couldn't force himself to clutter things up again. He asked me if I could—" She gestured. "Well, you see what I'm doing."

"Leave it," Hilary said, resting her chin in her hand. "I'll mess it up again soon enough." She pondered the effort Matt was making on her behalf.

Sheila reached for the coffeepot and poured herself a cup. "So what are you going to do this summer, now that your whale-watching plans have gone awry?"

"I haven't had a chance to give it much thought," Hilary answered. She stood and restlessly wandered about the kitchen, unconsciously moving things here and there so that they conformed to her own version of order. "I suppose I should get a job, at least a part-time one. On the other hand, I could spend the summer painting. I need to build up my inventory for the Plaza Art Fair in September."

"Every time you get a summer job you hate it," Sheila reminded her.

Hilary wrinkled her nose in agreement. She'd spent one summer sewing endless yards of canvas for an awning company. Another of her temporary jobs had been as a clerk in a specialty store selling garter belts and lacy chemises of questionable taste. Sheila was right. "But I do need the money,'' Hilary said aloud. ''I have to start saving for the MammalTrackers project next summer. They've promised me a volunteer slot if I want it.''

''The art fair should boost your finances,'' said Sheila. ''And you'll also be receiving rent from Matt. Hey, I know. Maybe you could do some work for him.''

Hilary awarded Sheila the laugh she saved for the most improbable jokes. ''Don't be ridiculous. Matt and I simply aren't cut from the same cloth. We could never work together.'' Even as she said the words, she winced at her own pessimism. Normally she wasn't so negative.

''He's really very nice,'' Sheila began, but Hilary held up her hand in protest.

''I know he's nice,'' she agreed, though she felt that ''nice'' was too bland a word to describe Matt. ''I'm the one who's put my worst face forward. It's just that I feel so tired and cranky from this pneumonia business. I start out trying to be friendly, but I'm afraid I don't have much patience dealing with his little surprises. Matt must think—''

''Matt must think what?''

Hilary turned to see the object of their conversation standing in the doorway. Though he was seven or eight feet away, she could almost feel him touching her. She'd never known a man with such a powerful presence.

When she failed to answer Matt's question, Sheila took up the slack. ''We were just discussing what Hilary might do for the rest of the summer, and I happened to mention that you—'' She cut herself off with a big sip of coffee. ''Well, it's none of my business, anyway. Listen, I have to run. I need to get lunch started. See you kids later!'' With a flourish she made her exit.

Matt squinted after his aunt, obviously confused. ''What was that all about?''

"That was a typical Sheila move. I was caught in the act of blatantly discussing you, and she was trying to save me from saying something embarrassing."

"Such as?" He raised one comical eyebrow at her.

Hilary sighed. "Pull up a chair and get yourself some coffee. C'mon," she added when he hesitated, "I know it's messy in here by your standards, but the clutter isn't catching. And I won't bite."

"Are you sure?"

Hilary detected a barely concealed smile beneath his words, and she allowed herself the luxury of genuine laughter. "I know I deserve that, so I won't rebuke you. Now sit down. Please."

He pulled out a chair and eased into it with the grace of a surefooted tomcat.

"You really surprised me when you showed up at the cemetery," she said. "I thought you'd be a little testier toward me after the way I've behaved."

Matt shrugged. "A little good-natured flippancy doesn't faze me. Anyway, I'm sure the shock of finding me here hasn't made your homecoming any easier. Now what were you going to say before I interrupted you? 'Matt must think . . .' what?" he prompted.

"That I'm not an altogether sweet person," Hilary admitted, studying him while trying to appear as if she were looking at her fingernails. "You haven't seen me at my best."

"Then I guess I have a treat in store for me."

There was nothing suggestive in what he said, but nonetheless, Matt's tone of voice gave Hilary a case of shivers. Or maybe it was the return of her fever; she wasn't quite sure.

"And what was Sheila babbling about before she ran out of here?" Matt asked. "Something about your plans for the rest of the summer?"

"You don't miss a beat, do you? She just thought you might have a job lead for me," Hilary hedged. That was the truth, more or less.

"I'm afraid the only job I know about isn't much. I usually hire a kid to help me part-time in the summer, but it's hard, hot work and I only pay minimum wage. That's probably not the most attractive job description you've ever heard."

Hilary sat up a little straighter. "Oh, I don't know. Most summer jobs don't pay much more than minimum wage, anyway. And this late in the season all the good jobs have been taken. I bet a lot of kids would be glad to work for you."

"And what about you?"

Hilary held her breath for a moment, then made what seemed a sensible response. "I don't think I'm remotely qualified."

"Why not? You're good with plants. If you're a teacher you must be a hard worker. Surely if you worked for MammalTrackers you can work for me."

"But I already told you I'm lousy at scientific stuff."

"I'll take care of the 'scientific stuff.' All I need is a helping hand. You'd be perfect."

Hilary was at a loss for words. Good sense told her to turn down the job and run the other way. She and Matt struck too many sparks between them to work together compatibly. But the idea of spending her summer puttering around in the greenhouse and garden was undeniably more appealing than sewing awnings.

"If you're offering, I'm taking," she finally said. Full speed ahead, and damn the torpedoes. "I never thought anyone would pay me to dig around in the dirt. When do you want me to start?''

Matt held up his hand. ''When you're rested and one hundred percent healthy again, and not a moment sooner. I expect you to spend at least a week in bed recuperating. No more of this running off to sit in a cemetery.''

''A week! You don't know me very well. I can't sit still for a day, let alone seven of them.''

''Consider it part of the employment offer.''

''I'll give you three days.''

''Five,'' Matt countered.

''Four. Do we have a deal?'' Hilary smiled and held out her hand. Matt grasped it, but the firm shake she expected never materialized. At the first contact of her skin to his, her smile faded and her whole body came alive with a quivering awareness. She knew Matt was affected, too. She could actually *feel* his surprise and uncertainty, almost as if the emotions were wafting across the airspace toward her.

They remained motionless, their hands clasped loosely, for uncounted seconds. She couldn't pull her eyes away from him.

Shaken, she finally drew her hand back, all but sitting on it to keep it from trembling. The moment passed and their conversation resumed in a normal fashion, but Hilary remembered the exchange for a long time afterward.

Chapter Three

Hilary bolted upright in bed, fully and uncomfortably awake. What was that ungodly noise, and at this hour? But when she looked at her clock radio, she discovered it wasn't all that early. She rose to her knees and peered out the window by the bed.

Matt. He was mowing the narrow strip of grass at the side of her house. Didn't he know Sunday mornings were for sleeping in? She opened the window and leaned out just as the sun slipped behind a cloud.

"Hey, do you have to do that right now? It's barely nine o'clock."

Matt paused at his efforts and looked up, then grinned sheepishly. "Sorry. I wanted to get this done before the heat..." His words trailed off and his grin faded, but his gaze remained steady.

Right about then Hilary became excruciatingly aware of her state of dishabille. She was leaning out the window in nothing but a camisole. She was aware of him, too—his wide shoulders pushing at the seams of the snug T-shirt he wore, his strong hands clenched around the lawn mower, and his dark eyes almost devouring her. She could feel a blush creeping over her entire body.

"I'm trying to sleep, so hurry it up," she ordered curtly before retreating inside and slamming the window shut, her heart beating like a jackhammer.

It was a cinch she'd never get back to sleep, not after that rude awakening, Hilary thought as the adrenaline continued to pump through her veins. She might as well get up.

She stretched her arms over her head and took a deep breath, noting the absence of tightness in her chest. After four days of recuperative lethargy, it was time to rejoin the human race. She'd take a steaming hot shower and get an early start on the day.

Her thoughts remained on Matt as she turned on the shower faucet. Though she hadn't seen much of him over the past few days, she was reminded of his presence in a thousand little ways—fresh towels in the bathroom, a neatly folded newspaper on the kitchen table. And a lawn mower under her window, she reminded herself when she caught her own smile in the mirror. Shaking her head, she stepped into the shower.

An icy blast of water spewed out of the faucet just as Hilary got her hair lathered. Her roommate had obviously beaten her to the bath, she seethed as she shivered under the glacial spray. Another little reminder of his presence.

One thing was certain: her feelings toward Matt were anything but neutral. They ran as hot and cold as her shower.

Determinedly brushing her irritation away, she turned off the water, blotted herself dry and applied her favorite dusting powder. In light of the warmer weather that had descended on Kansas City, she dressed in a pair of striped cotton slacks, cropped just below the knee, and a sleeveless T-shirt in muted green. She applied a hint of makeup, then fussed with her uncooperative hair until it framed her face in soft, coppery waves.

Physically she felt strong and healthy, for the first time in a week. She wanted to look good, too.

On the way out the bedroom door, she paused to study herself in the full-length mirror. Was she just feeling her oats? Or was she blatantly primping to impress Matt?

Matt deserved to see her at her best after what she'd subjected him to so far, she rationalized. She stubbornly refused to admit that her preening was in any way related to the feminine courtship ritual.

Satisfied with her appearance and determined to steer the day into smoother waters, she turned from the mirror and headed downstairs, whistling slightly off-key.

As he stood over the rosebushes with a hose, Matt thought of Hilary for at least the twentieth time that morning, then cursed softly in irritation. Over the past few days he'd caught only an occasional, breathtaking glimpse of her—like this morning, when the sun had peeked out from behind a cloud and suddenly illuminated her figure beneath her white camisole. But thoughts of her had disturbed his peace of mind more times than he'd like to admit. At night, especially, as he contorted his body to fit the too-small bed, he thought about her sleeping in that roomy four-poster across the hall and had to bite his knuckles to keep from groaning aloud.

Why her, and why now? His solitary life, perfectly satisfying until this week, suddenly looked damned sterile.

He'd tried to categorize all of her qualities, thinking that if he summed up the positive and negative on paper he'd be able to understand the almost unbearably strong pull she had on him, and then conquer it.

She wasn't a knockout in the looks department. She was only passably pretty, in a wild, earthy sort of way. But he liked the way she looked, even without the artifice of makeup. He'd give her one point for natural prettiness . . . and a bonus for her legs.

She was also intelligent, witty, and tough. Three more points. On the down side, she was undeniably bossy and often sharp-tongued. He subtracted points.

When he was done with his mental accounting, he reviewed it, but it offered no clues. He couldn't put his finger on any trait that alone could cause Hilary to stand so far apart from other women he knew.

When he caught sight of her crossing the patio in his direction, he revised his opinion about her looks. She wasn't just passably pretty. She could steal a man's breath right out of his lungs.

What had possessed him to hire her as an assistant? he asked himself, not for the first time. She would distract him unmercifully.

"Good morning," she greeted him, cheerfully oblivious of his turmoil.

"Feeling better, are we?" Her unexpected smile had softened his brain, and the scent of her teased his imagination.

"I feel great. In fact, I feel so good that I'm going to forgive you for jolting me out of bed and invite you to breakfast. French toast. Interested?"

"Am I allowed in the kitchen?" The question reeked with friendly suspicion.

Hilary shoved her hands in her pockets and glanced down at the tips of her white sandals. "I'm trying to make a peaceful gesture here. The least you could do is—excuse me, but do you always water the roof?"

Matt turned his attention toward the stream of water issuing from the forgotten garden hose in his hands. He was indeed soaking the roof of the garage. Quickly he redirected the spray toward the rosebushes. "Roof garden," he mumbled.

"What?"

"Never mind. Did you see the new blooms?"

"Rose blooms?" Hilary shifted her attention toward the four bushes, which now each sported exactly one fat, flowering bud. Slowly a smile spread across her face as she considered a wealth of mystifying factors that might have caused the roses to suddenly rejoice in the unique way only they could. "That's certainly an improvement." She bent closer to one of the pale pink blossoms and inhaled, then began speaking in hushed tones.

Matt leaned closer to catch her words.

"Mmm, you smell so sweet," she said in a sibilant whisper. "I'm so proud of you for putting forth this effort."

It took Matt a moment to realize she was actually talking to the flowers. "It would make more sense to thank the gardener," he said softly, his lips perilously close to her ear. "At least the gardener can hear."

Hilary started, straightened, and took an instinctive step backward when the spray from the hose threatened to douse her. Her green eyes were full of challenges, and not all of them had to do with their conversation about flowers.

"I wouldn't be such a doubter if I were you, at least not right in front of them." She nodded toward the roses.

"They're liable to turn on you. Those thorns can be pretty sharp."

"I've got a sturdy pair of gloves," he shot back, barely controlling his laughter. "But let's not argue. You believe what you like. Do you really want to fix breakfast?"

Instantly the warmth returned to Hilary's expression. "Sure. I'll go in and get things started. Come on in when you're done drowning things out here." Having gotten in the last word, she spun around and walked away with a jaunty stride.

Matt looked down. A lake was forming at the base of the bushes where the water had gushed unnoticed during the last few minutes. Dammit it, he *would* drown the poor bushes if he wasn't careful. It wasn't like him to absentmindedly let his attention drift from the task at hand.

He turned off the water and shook his head. He could see more clearly than ever that allowing Hilary McShane near his greenhouse was inviting trouble. His work depended on strict attention to detail and exacting controls. Letting his mind wander could be disastrous.

He could still change his mind, he supposed, and tell Hilary she'd have to find another job. Briefly he pressed his fingers against his forehead. No, he wouldn't go back on his word. He'd just have to quit wanting her; that was all there was to it. If he stuck close to her until he was accustomed to her alluring presence, eventually she would lose the power to distract him.

When he entered the kitchen a few minutes later, he had to bite his tongue to keep from groaning. The countertop was littered with eggshells, bread crumbs, coffee grounds, paper towels, and an empty orange juice can.

He quickly schooled his face—but not before Hilary turned away from the eggs she was beating and caught a glimpse of his initial amazement.

"Just don't say anything," she warned. "This is the way I cook. Nothing I fix comes out right if I don't make a mess."

"I wasn't going to say a thing." Matt found himself a juice glass and filled it from a pitcher in the refrigerator. "Is there anything I can do to help?" Surely, he thought, if she had some assistance she would have time to discover the trash can and use it.

"No, I've got everything under control," she answered breezily. "Just have a seat and—oh, you can clear some of that newspaper away. Or help yourself to whatever section you want."

Matt located the sports section and settled down to read about the Royals, even though he'd attended yesterday's game. But he found himself peering over the top of the paper at Hilary's back instead. As she vigorously whipped the eggs, her derriere took up an intriguing oscillation.

"How many pieces would you like?" she asked.

Matt jumped at her question, then realized she was talking about French toast.

"A couple would be fine," he answered as his heartbeat resumed a normal pace. "I don't usually eat a large breakfast."

"I don't, either. In fact, during the week I settle for fruit or yogurt, or maybe a piece of toast. But Sundays are different. My grandmother always fixed something full of calories and cholesterol for breakfast, and I've carried on the tradition, though it's not as much fun when there's nobody to share it with."

Matt put down the paper and gave up all pretense of reading. "Don't you ever have...guests on Sunday mornings?" He asked the question in such a way that she couldn't fail to catch his meaning. It was none of his business, but he couldn't seem to stop himself from trying to find out.

She didn't seem put off by the question, but she did hesitate before answering. "No, no Sunday morning guests. No regular guest sleeping over Saturday nights, either. I assume that *is* what you're asking."

He shouldn't have felt such relief. Things would be infinitely easier if Hilary did have a man in her life. The fact that she didn't only made it more difficult to resist her. He studied her with a renewed interest as she gently settled the egg-soaked bread into the hot frying pan.

"What about you?" she asked as she put more bread into the bowl of batter. "Is there anyone in your life who might object to your new living arrangements—innocent though they are?"

Right, innocent, Matt thought with a small stab of guilt. "No, no girlfriend. No wife, no lover. I'm afraid my current life-style just isn't conducive to relationships. I work alone too much, I guess, so I don't socialize much. What's your excuse?"

"Pardon?"

"Why aren't you married? Or something."

He expected her to laugh at his blunt question. Instead, indecisiveness crossed her face, as if she wasn't sure she should reveal her thoughts on the subject.

"I'm just not the type of person to get married," she finally said with a dismissive wave of her hand.

"Why not?" he pushed, inexplicably consumed with a need to know.

She flipped the toast before answering. "Marriage means settling down," she explained. "I can't see myself doing that, now or ever. I have too much living left to do. Lord only knows where I'll be next year, or even next month. What husband would put up with me?"

Matt gave her a teasing smile. "Surely you could find some man to tolerate you, if you put your mind to it."

"No." The definite tone of her answer surprised him, as did her sudden, sharp frown that came and went in a heartbeat. "No, I wouldn't even want to try."

Matt resumed his perusal of the newspaper, feigning an interest in baseball. He'd inadvertently pushed the wrong button when he'd teased her. She'd reacted as if she'd been scalded.

"How much toast did you say you wanted?" she asked, her tone neutral.

"Two pieces." He put the paper in front of his face again to hide his consternation.

They ate their breakfast with little conversation. Hilary's stream of friendly talk had halted abruptly. She sat quietly across the table from Matt, daintily eating her French toast without dripping a single drop of syrup on her chin, the table or even her plate.

A messy cook but a neat eater, Matt concluded. He was so absorbed in watching her that he failed to notice the huge glop of syrup rolling off the edge of his own fork. He caught it just in time with the end of his little finger. Reflexively he stuck his syrup-coated pinkie into his mouth.

When he looked back up, Hilary was staring at him, mesmerized. Her eyes were large and smoky, her mouth was open just slightly, and her fork had frozen in midair. The tip of her pink tongue flicked at the corner of her lips.

He thought for a moment that he could hear her heartbeat, but it had to be his own.

Fresh air. He needed some breathing room. "It was a wonderful breakfast, Hilary. Thank you." He stood abruptly and took his plate to the sink, then quickly excused himself.

Hilary made some vague parting comment. Then she just sat staring at her half-eaten toast, wondering why breakfast had turned into such a strange affair.

The inane talk of marriage had gotten things off to a shaky start. She hadn't meant for the conversation to turn so serious, but her decision not to marry wasn't something she took lightly. She'd been tempted once, not so long ago. But the closer she'd come to the altar, the louder her grandmother's voice had echoed in her head.

"You're so much like your mother it's frightening, Hilary," she'd once said. "You're a free spirit, a wanderer. You do as you please, when and where you please. There's nothing wrong with that, as long as you realize you'll never change. And you must never let any man try to convince you that you *can* change. I know. I watched your mother's heart break when she tried and failed to be the wife your father wanted."

Apparently Grandma had been right. Stephen had tried to reform Hilary, to turn her into a good little wife even before he'd slipped the noose over her head. Thank God she'd realized it in time.

She still couldn't see herself married to any man, not really. What man *would* sit still while his wife wandered off to Alaska for three months to watch whales?

Her mind drifted of its own accord to the evocative image of Matt licking syrup off his finger. Her pulse raced even at the memory. Once again, the fates were drawing her toward a supremely improbable man.

She was glad Matt had slipped away when he did, she decided, or she might have grabbed his hand and licked some of that syrup herself. But it struck her as odd that he hadn't even offered to help with the dishes.

At eight sharp the next morning, Hilary showed up at the L-shaped greenhouse in her khaki shorts and a yellow camp shirt, ready to work. She was eager to get her hands into some dirt. She'd refrained from planting a garden this year because she'd thought she'd be away all summer. She hadn't realized until now how much she missed her contact with the earth.

She was smiling in anticipation as she reached for the greenhouse door. But the smile fell flat as she entered the glass building. Of course she should have expected it, knowing Matt as she already did, but the sight of all those precise rows of flats and ruler-straight lines of pots surprised her anyway. Clipboards were suspended on nails in front of each grouping of small plants. Meticulously labeled plastic bottles full of colored liquids sat on the overhead shelves. And not a leaf was out of place.

Hilary thought of how the greenhouse had looked last spring, filled with herbage growing lush and out of control. Now it looked like a concentration camp for plants.

She heard Matt making noises around the corner—sweeping noises, if she guessed correctly. Her heart seemed to expand and contract too quickly at the prospect of facing him again, but a quick, silent reprimand brought her physiology under control.

Just as she'd expected, she found him in the other corridor going after minuscule particles of dirt with his well-heeled broom.

He looked up, his expression all business. "I take it you're ready for work?"

"Yup." To avoid looking into those dark, knowing eyes of his, she glanced around once more at the rigid arrangement. Then, carefully, she said, "You've changed a few things in here."

"Organized, you mean?"

"Well, yeah. I've never seen a greenhouse this neat." Absently she picked up one of the small square pots and studied the healthy sprout. "What's this?"

"That's a Fall Surprise tomato."

"But it's already almost June. Isn't it too late for a tomato to be in a pot?"

"Not this one. By the end of July we'll have the first mature fruit, and it'll keep producing up to the first freeze. These tomatoes have an incredible storage capacity. It's an excellent variety for procrastinators."

"You sound just like a seed catalog."

"That's the idea. But never mind the plants right now. We need to have a talk."

"Oh? What about?" She started to put the pot down, but Matt wrapped his own large hands around it and replaced it himself. She realized she'd been about to set it down in the wrong spot.

"About just that. Organization. It's important—crucial—in the greenhouse. Everything has to stay in its proper place, so that each plant gets its prescribed program."

"Program? What do you do, put them through aerobics?"

His eyes crinkled at the edges and a dimple tried to form at the corner of his mouth as he suppressed a laugh. "This is serious," he reminded her, though the almost-smile ruined his attempt at sternness. "I have this little speech I have to get through, and then we can start work."

Hilary schooled her face. "All right, no more jokes. Make your speech. I'm all ears."

"Thank you. You see, I'm at the final stage of testing with this group of seeds," he explained. "My job is to figure out under what conditions the average gardener can make the plants produce. So I work with variables such as soil, water, fertilizer and light. The program for each group of plants is recorded on the clipboards. You have to follow the directions exactly, and—" He looked at her pointedly. "Be very careful not to mix up the plants." His smile softened the admonishment.

Hilary nodded, responding more to the smile than the warning. "All right, I understand. And I hereby duly swear not to treat the greenhouse like my kitchen. Everything will remain in its proper place."

"Then we'll have no problems. Come on, I'll give you the grand tour."

Hilary spent the rest of the morning getting acquainted with the various seedlings and their "programs." She found she had to concentrate very hard on Matt's words, for her attention tended to stray every so often to his tanned, well-muscled legs revealed so eloquently by snug cutoffs faded almost to white. She approved of his ultracasual wardrobe. He might be neat, and he might be a scientist, but he wasn't stuffy.

Matt had started the seedlings deliberately late in the season, he explained. He was serious—the Fall Surprise was a variety especially for procrastinators. At this point the plants appeared mature enough to Hilary to be put out in the garden with the exception of one group of flats.

"What are these?" she asked, pointing to the seedlings no bigger than the tip of her finger, just peeking above the surface of the sandy planting medium.

"They're roses, believe it or not."

Hilary was pleasantly surprised. So he *did* have an affinity for roses. Maybe that's why her bushes responded to him. "You didn't tell me you hybridized roses as well."

"It's just a hobby. I haven't met with much success, but it's still entertaining to cross two flowers and see what comes of it."

"Grandma used to do the same thing. She even won a prize at a regional flower show for a rose she developed."

"What sort of rose was it?" Matt asked, his curiosity aroused. Chances were one in a thousand that an amateur could develop a truly unique, patentable plant, though sometimes back-yard fanciers did beat the odds.

"It was gorgeous," Hilary answered, "pale yellow with a dark orange center. She called it Spring Sunrise. I've never seen anything like it."

"Did she try to go commercial with it?"

Hilary shrugged. "Not that I know of. She wasn't particularly interested in making money. She just grew it and enjoyed it, and eventually she gave it away to one of her friends. She gave away almost all of her roses when she became ill, except for the pink ones."

"It's not easy to develop a distinct hybrid, you know," Matt commented. "I don't suppose you have any pictures of this Spring Sunrise, do you?"

"Oh, I probably do, though I'm not sure where. Maybe the old photo albums are down in the basement."

"Uh, that's okay, it's not important," Matt said quickly. He wanted to postpone Hilary's visit to the basement for as long as possible. He'd cleaned it up before she'd put a freeze on organization, and he had no idea how she'd react when she saw the dramatic change.

He and Hilary were finally making a stab at cordiality, and he had no intention of jeopardizing their truce.

Thankfully she dropped the subject of her grandmother's rose.

They spent most of the day outdoors, tilling the garden soil for several test patches Matt wanted to plant, preparing each bed with a different mixture of fertilizer. It felt good to work her muscles, Hilary decided, even if it was a trifle hot. Before too many minutes had passed, she'd pulled her curly hair into a ponytail and tied her cotton shirt into a knot below her breasts, to bare her midriff.

Matt had gone further than that. He'd discarded his T-shirt and now wore nothing but the brief cutoffs. Several times Hilary caught herself leaning on her long-handled cultivator, lost in fantasy, watching the muscles of his sweat-glistened back bunching and relaxing as he worked. He really was a magnificent specimen, she conceded, even better than she'd thought after the glimpse she'd caught of his almost-naked body the first night they'd met. His skin was tan and smooth, his shoulders wide, his legs firm and athletic-looking with just a dusting of dark, springy hair.

He certainly didn't look the way she imagined a horticulturist ought to look.

"Hilary, would you mind getting one more of those green bags of fertilizer?"

His request broke through her reverie. Grateful for a chance to sneak herself a drink from the hose in the greenhouse, she nodded to him and hurried to fetch the bag of fertilizer. She didn't approve of it because it wasn't strictly organic, but she supposed it wasn't her place to argue.

The greenhouse was hot, despite the fact that all the vents were open and the fans running. Hilary made her way down one arm of the L and halfway down the other, pausing in front of the faucet. Her mouth was parched. She turned on the hose, waited a few moments until she got a cool stream, then bent her head and touched her lips to the water. She took several swallows, then splashed some of the welcome moisture onto her face and around the back of her neck.

Matt would be thirsty too, she thought. After she brought him the fertilizer, she'd see about getting both of them some ice water from the house.

She took one more sip of water before reaching to turn the faucet off. Then she noticed the wilted seedlings. Two trays full of small tomato plants were positively withering.

"Oh, you poor things," she said, turning down the volume of water so that she could dribble a gentle stream into each of the pots.

She'd already watered three of them when a niggling apprehension caused her to stop and think. *Oh, no, Hilary, what have you done?* She held the hose back and looked at the clipboards that hung in front of each flat. It was just as she'd suspected; these plants were on strict water rations. They were being tested for drought resistance.

Thank God she hadn't watered all of them. Quickly she picked up each of the small pots she's watered and dumped out as much liquid as she could, murmuring, "Sorry, babies. You'll have to go thirsty." She quickened her movements when she heard the greenhouse door open.

"Hilary?" Matt called as he made his way down the corridor. "What's the matter, can't you find the right fertilizer? It's on the top shelf, right over the—" His words halted as he came around the corner, and a black scowl overtook his face.

"Sorry I was taking so long," Hilary hastened to explain. "I stopped to get a drink and then—"

"Just what the hell do you think you're doing?" he roared, grabbing the hose out of her hand.

She snatched it right back. "Don't look so stricken. I caught my mistake before it got out of hand."

Again, he took the hose out of her hands. "What did I just say this morning? Hilary—"

"I know, I know. I only watered a couple of them before I remembered to check the clipboards."

His expression grew even more severe, if that were possible. He reached out to turn off the faucet, then dropped the hose. The brass nozzle clinked when it hit the concrete floor, the noise echoing against the glass walls. "Of all the brainless—"

"When a plant looks thirsty, I automatically water it. It's a reflex action." She faced him defiantly, hands on hips, chin thrust out. "I told you, the scientific method and I don't get along. You're the one who said I was qualified for this job. Why don't you just fire me and get it over with?"

"Throttling you would give me a great deal more satisfaction." He took a couple of threatening steps toward her.

She stood her ground. "It was a *small* mistake, Matthew. I suppose you can fire me over it, but if you call me brainless again I'll knock your block off," she added in an even voice.

His hands went to her shoulders, but they were strangely gentle. All the anger seemed to have drained from his face.

Hilary felt her outrage dissipating, too, as something else took its place. Matt's hands, with which he'd so recently threatened to throttle her, now moved in a caressing motion along her shoulders, then up either side of her neck, until he framed her damp face between his palms.

"Damn it, Hilary, what's happening here?" he whispered just before his lips took hers in a harsh kiss.

Hilary hadn't realized how truly thirsty she was, and she drank in the headiness of Matt's touch, his taste, his sweaty but welcome male scent. Her hands were trapped between them, resting on his bare chest. She flattened her palms against the warm flesh, then eased her hands around in a slow caress until they were on his back, pulling him closer.

She could taste the salt of perspiration and the trace of Matt's morning coffee. She felt his callused thumbs grazing her cheeks, sending shivers all the way to the soles of her feet. Her own frenzied breathing echoed in her ears. The tips of her breasts barely touched his chest. She ached to press harder and flatten them against him.

The kiss gentled, evolving into a soft give and take, until Matt pulled away. He tipped her head back, searching her eyes for an answer she didn't have.

"I'm sorry about the water," she ventured. Her voice cracked.

"Forget about the damn water. I want to know what just happened."

"That was what's known as a kiss." Her cavalier comment did little to lessen the significance of what had just passed between them.

"It was more than that," Matt insisted.

"Just because you're a scientist doesn't mean you have to analyze everything." She smiled faintly, but her expression was met with one of confusion.

Abruptly he released her. "I hope you don't think that was some kind of macho domination attempt on my part because I was angry. The one had nothing to do with the other."

"If I'd thought that, I would have ended it with a well-placed knee."

That finally got a grudging grin out of Matt. "I don't doubt that for a minute."

"And I hope you don't think I . . . participated so you wouldn't fire me," Hilary quickly added. "I'll even resign if you want. I'm not cut out to be a horticulturist's assistant."

"You're not fired, and I won't let you quit." To her surprise, he reached for the hose, turned on the faucet and let the gushing water cascade over his head. She watched in fascination as rivulets trickled over his bare skin and soaked the faded denim of his shorts. "But please, don't do *anything* to the plants until you check the clipboards first."

"I won't. Promise." She waited for him to finish his impromptu shower before saying anything further. The kiss had left her hot and vibrating with passion, and while she didn't expect Matt to slake that passion, she wanted to know what was going on between them just as much as he did.

But to her disappointment, he dropped the hose, turned his back and walked out on her.

Chapter Four

Tuesday morning dawned gray, humid and uncomfortably warm. A steady precipitation fell short of refreshing, so Matt had to settle for muggy. At least the rain took care of watering the test garden, he thought, but that left him with precious little to occupy himself.

Even after leaving a note for Hilary giving her the day off, Matt had completed his work in the greenhouse by midmorning. That left only some computer work. He might be able to fill his day with that, he thought ruefully as he gazed at the pitiful amount he'd accomplished so far. In the three hours he'd been sitting at the desk in his small bedroom, he'd typed in exactly seventeen words.

Normally he enjoyed this part of his work—synthesizing his notes and measurements into a coherent report for his seed company client. Today, however, he simply couldn't muster the necessary concentration. He would no more than start to type when his hands would slow over the keyboard and his mind would wander to the images that had haunted him late into the previous night, then almost constantly since he'd awakened this morning.

Hilary.

All he could think about was her soft red-gold hair, smooth as mink against his face, and her firm body, which had felt so right pressed against the length of his. She'd carried the scent of soap and garden soil when he'd kissed her, and somehow she'd made the fragrance more sexy than the priciest perfume.

What had possessed him to reach for her in the first place? One moment he'd been mad enough to wring her neck, and the next.... His behavior had been impulsive, imprudent, and inappropriate. What was worse, it violated a personal philosophy he'd lived by for almost ten years.

The philosophy wasn't something he took lightly. In college he'd suffered through a singularly disastrous affair with a gorgeous but flighty phys-ed student. They'd shared few interests outside the physical plane, yet Matt had been obsessed with her for eight weeks of his life. During those eight weeks, he'd blown his grade point average and lost a scholarship. After that he'd sworn never to let a chance physical attraction overrule his common sense.

He'd had no trouble living by that philosophy. Until now.

He should have doused himself with the hose *before* he ever thought of kissing Hilary. Still, when his active imagination replayed that brief but electrifying moment, Matt found himself tamping down an unfamiliar sense of elation.

He couldn't help wondering what Hilary thought of his behavior. At the time she'd seemed pretty sure of herself, even casual about the kiss. Almost cavalier. As though she were kissed every day. That thought gave birth to a whole slew of confusing feelings and images.

He didn't like being confused. He liked things clear and concise and predictable.

One prediction he could make with utter certainty: he wouldn't kiss her again. He couldn't go through another day like this, literally afraid to face her, guilty, jittery, and strung as tight as a bowstring.

With that conviction firmly in mind, he refocused his attention on his computer screen. He'd just completed his first truly coherent sentence when an ominous rumble of thunder caused him to sigh in defeat. If an electrical storm was threatening, he had to turn off his computer and unplug it or risk a bolt of lightning zapping his report into another dimension.

He closed his file and flipped the switch to "off." Then he began to pace the room, much too small for pacing. Desperate for something to do, he'd just about decided to drive to Blue Springs and check on the progress of the remodeling at his house when a soft tapping sounded at his door.

"Matt, are you in there?"

He had to face her eventually. He opened the door and managed an uneasy smile. "Hi."

"Hi yourself."

His memory hadn't done her justice, he thought as he took in her faded jeans and cropped T-shirt. She'd pulled her hair back in a loose braid that hung sassily over one shoulder. The effect was nothing short of devastating.

"I just heard a weather report," she was saying. "Some marble-sized hail is headed our way, and I was worried about the garden."

The threat of hail mobilized him. His mind, which had felt so sludgy all day, clicked into gear. "I suppose we'd better take some precautions," he agreed. "Put your raincoat on and meet me out back. I'll get some empty boxes from the basement."

"Need any help toting them up?" she asked over her shoulder as he followed her downstairs.

"No," he answered hastily, still hoping to keep her out of the basement for as long as possible.

A few minutes later he met Hilary on the patio with an armload of flattened boxes and a roll of packing tape. "Where's your raincoat?" he asked as they stood sheltered from the downpour by the overhang and made short work of popping the cartons open and taping the bottoms shut.

"Oh, I think I lost it in Alaska," she replied breezily. "But I don't mind a little rain." She gave his yellow slicker a once-over before grabbing two of the boxes and darting out to the garden. She carefully placed the cardboard shelters over a group of the fragile plants.

With a shrug Matt followed her example. By the time they were done with the task a few minutes later, rain had soaked Hilary's clothes, and her formerly sassy braid straggled limply down her back. Matt could feel his own hair plastered to his forehead and rain dripping down the inside of his collar. His shoes sloshed on the inside.

The light exertion had quickened Hilary's breath, and her eyes glittered with mischief as she smiled at their bedraggled state. He was about to give her an answering smile when he abruptly remembered her illness. Great

Scott, what had he been thinking, allowing her to run about in the rain with no protection?

"Get inside and dry yourself off before you have a relapse," he said gruffly.

"I don't think there's any danger of that," Hilary argued good-naturedly as she opened the patio door, wiped her feet on the doormat and stepped inside. "It's as warm out as a steam bath. As a matter of fact, the rain felt warmer than my shower this morning."

"Just the same, a change of clothes couldn't hurt," he said as he followed her through her studio and into the downstairs bath. Her damp T-shirt delineated the curves of her back to perfection, and he found himself half hoping she wouldn't dry off any time soon.

The enticing view was obscured for a few moments as he used his towel to dry the moisture from his face and neck. When he looked at her again, she had turned and was staring back at him, her smoky green eyes alive with curiosity.

"You've been avoiding me," she commented casually.

He looked at her sharply, alarmed at the sudden turn of their conversation. He hadn't meant to be so obvious in his efforts to keep away from her. "I guess I have been giving you a wide berth."

"Why?"

He had to give this some thought before answering. He wasn't sure why, unless it was that he'd hoped time and distance would put things into perspective. "I wanted to cool off and think about things," he finally answered.

"And have you?" She perched on the arm of the couch and pulled the elastic band out of her hair. In an effort to avoid her eyes, Matt focused on the motions of her hands as she unraveled her wet braid. They trembled slightly, giving lie to her outward calmness.

"I've thought about all kinds of things," he answered truthfully. "Mostly I've thought about what a jerk I was. And I want to...to apologize." The words sounded stiff even to him, and he realized that he wasn't accustomed to justifying his actions to anyone. "I overreacted when I saw you'd watered those plants," he continued when she offered him a perplexed expression. "I shouldn't have expected perfection from you, not the first day."

"Apology accepted," she said, nodding her head regally. "But we both know your short temper isn't the whole issue here."

She wasn't going to let the matter drop gracefully. She challenged him with a look that said so.

"I assume you're referring to the kiss," he said resignedly. "I was hoping we could forget it, put it behind us."

"Why?" she asked again in that infernally direct way of hers.

Didn't she realize that some things were best not put into words? How could he explain that she scared the stuffing out of him? Her innate sensuality brought out a side of him that was strange, uncontrollable, and thus downright dangerous. Even now, a dark part of him wanted to grab hold of her, pull her close, and kiss her until reason departed and these painful explanations weren't necessary.

"Why do you want to forget it?" she repeated when he didn't answer. Her voice was softer now, almost wistful, certainly not challenging as before.

He did his best to provide a logical, unemotional explanation. "I'm your tenant. You're my employee. It's not professional. It's not prudent. And it won't happen again."

Hilary was silent for a time. She stared at a point somewhere above Matt's left shoulder as she finger-combed her tangled hair. "What if you weren't my tenant, and I wasn't your employee," she offered tentatively. "At the end of the summer—"

"Look, Hilary," he interrupted, wanting to head off her all-too-sensible argument before she could start it. "I don't want to be blunt. But on a personal level, you and I are completely, irrevocably incompatible."

"For heaven's sake, we aren't applying for a marriage license," she argued reasonably.

He refused to be moved by logic. That was his arena, anyway. How dare she use it against him?

"All right," she said in the face of his stoic silence, "I get the message. No use beating my head against a brick wall, right?" She stood and made an unexpectedly quick exit, leaving her damp towel draped over the arm of the sofa. Sitting alone in the den, Matt knew he should feel relief. He didn't.

Hilary cursed Matt's sensible nature as she made her way upstairs. She'd wanted to clear the air and she'd done it, all right—cleared it right into a vacuum. Dammit, the moment Matt had kissed her the world had tipped crazily, and nothing had been the same for her since. Didn't he feel it, too?

Apparently not. He had sounded undeniably definite just now. She tried to ignore the stab of disappointment that pierced her. She hadn't counted on this unequivocal rejection.

He was right, she supposed. They *were* incompatible—hideously so. She was reminded of it every time she looked in the refrigerator and saw how he'd rearranged the jars and bottles on the door. He'd put all the jellies and jams on one shelf, the mustards, mayonnaise and salad dressing on another.

That habit was just one of many obstacles that would stand in the way of harmony. Never mind that they enjoyed each other's company. Never mind that the physical spark that flared between them was enough to launch a space shuttle. Never mind that he was the most maddeningly fascinating man she'd ever met.

"That's not enough for the long haul, is it, Grandma," she said to the framed photo on her wall as she peeled off her damp T-shirt. She shivered and noticed she was goose bumps from head to toe. Her wet clothes had given her a chill. Curse the man, did he always have to be right?

The predicted hail never materialized. By six o'clock, the sun was shining, the puddles were drying, and a cool breeze from the north made the humidity bearable. Also at six o'clock, the Kansas City Royals were getting ready for a home game.

Matt plucked two tickets from an envelope he kept in his desk drawer, thinking that a rousing game of baseball was just the thing to get his mind off Hilary.

As soon as he could safely conclude that the game wouldn't be rained out, he ventured downstairs with his address book to use the kitchen phone. He didn't think he'd have a problem finding someone to go with him even at this late hour, given the picture-perfect way the day was turning out.

He was wrong.

He'd never found his group of fellow baseball enthusiasts so inaccessible. Stan was out of town. Mike had pulled a muscle in his back. Darryl had to attend a graduation. The list of excuses seemed interminable.

Matt finally resorted to calling Sheila and requesting the company of her son Bryan, who at age ten was just civilized enough to be tolerated, on a good day. But Bryan was getting ready for a softball game of his own.

"What about Bob?" Matt asked, referring to Sheila's husband.

"Don't even think about it," she said. "This is the first evening Bob and I have had alone in weeks. Meredith is out on a date, crutches and all, and the twins are baby-sitting. I just put some steaks on the grill, the wine is breathing, and if you drag Bob away—"

"All right, Sheila, I get the picture."

"Why don't you take Hilary with you?" Sheila asked casually.

Hilary was the last person he wanted to deal with right now. "Oh, I'm sure she's busy," he said in a dismissive tone.

"Why don't I ask her? She's standing right here."

"Uh, wait, Sheila—" He was too late.

"Sure, tell him I'd love to go," he heard Hilary saying a little too cheerfully in the background.

"See there?" said Sheila to Matt. "You should have just asked her in the first place. She loves baseball. Now say thank you, and then I have to go turn the steaks."

"Thanks, Aunt Sheila," he said dutifully before hanging up.

He was surprised Hilary had agreed to the outing. He'd done a pretty thorough job of rebuffing her, he thought with a stab of guilt, and he wouldn't have blamed her if she'd given him the cold shoulder. But apparently she'd decided to be gracious.

The more he thought about it, the more optimistic about the evening he felt. He and Hilary had to start somewhere if they wanted to reestablish their nice, safe friendship. A baseball game, with fifty thousand people all around them, sounded like the ideal place.

Hilary couldn't help but wonder how she'd survive the evening as she changed her clothes yet again, this time choosing a matching shorts outfit in a wild Hawaiian print. She had agreed to go to this game as a matter of principle, to show Matt that his rejection hadn't scared her off—not that she intended to pursue him, of course. If he didn't want to explore the feelings that were trying to bud between them, that was his choice.

He would no doubt be determined to have a lousy time, just to prove he was right about their incompatibility, but she was just as determined to have some fun. She wasn't a devoted Royals fan, despite what Sheila had told Matt, but if the game got boring she could always stuff herself silly with red-hots, roasted peanuts and cold beer.

When she emerged from her room, she found Matt waiting for her at the bottom of the stairs wearing his Royals cap, binoculars around his neck, and a little boy's expression of anticipation on his face. Something told her the evening wouldn't be boring after all.

He surprised her first by driving his Saab a consistent ten miles over the speed limit, zooming through changing yellow lights and switching lanes every few seconds with the precision of an Indy driver.

"Are we late?" she finally asked, trying to determine why he was in such a hurry.

"Huh? Oh, no. Sorry, I'll slow down. I just don't want to miss the opening pitch. McCommas is pitching, and he's always hottest during the first inning."

"You're a real Royals fanatic, then?" she asked, turning in her seat and leaning toward him slightly so that he could catch her words over the wind whipping through the sunroof.

He nodded. "Everyone's got to have one vice. Some people drink, some people gamble. I'm addicted to baseball games. It takes a genuine disaster to keep me away."

Hilary didn't doubt it. He was probably as compulsive about baseball as he was about organization. He probably kept his own statistics during the game.

After they'd parked the car in a remote space where the threat of dents or scratches was far removed, Matt reached into his glove compartment and pulled out a tiny radio with earphone.

"Don't tell me you listen to the game on the radio!" Hilary objected, amazed at the depth of his devotion to the game.

"How else would I get a decent commentary?" he asked.

She shook her head. This was a side to Matthew Burke she'd never seen.

Again Matt surprised her when they'd found their seats and the game against the Texas Rangers got underway. He drank beer and scarfed down a messy tray of nachos like a true baseball devotee. He even yelled at the umpire and in general seemed to have a riotously good time. He was more relaxed and at ease than she'd ever seen him. And, thank God, he didn't keep statistics.

It turned out to be a close, high-scoring game, but Hilary spent more time watching Matt than she did the proceedings on the field. She'd never seen anyone extract so much excitement out of a simple sporting event. What was more, the excitement was contagious. She could feel her own heart racing, her skin tingling. She stood on tiptoes and reached for the sky during the seventh-inning stretch. As the game resumed, she cracked open a roasted peanut, popped it into her mouth, then grinned into the wind for no apparent reason.

With the score tied at the bottom of the eighth, all of the spectators in their section were standing up. One particularly enthusiastic fan was waving his arms so wildly that his beer kept sloshing over the sides of the cup and splattering uncomfortably close to Hilary. Matt glanced over and, seeing her dilemma, grinned an apology for their rude neighbor and made room for Hilary to stand closer to him. She was grateful for his consideration, but the enforced closeness only made her more aware of him as a man. Their thighs were almost touching. She could sense his body heat and the smell of his earthy after-shave.

The longer she stood close to him, the more difficult she found it to keep her mind on the game. All she could think about was smoothing her palms over the hard plains of muscle beneath his soft cotton shirt, or nuzzling that little tuft of hair that sprang invitingly out of his open collar.

The whole stadium vibrated with cheering when the Royals pulled ahead by one run. Hilary forced herself to pay attention as the other team went to bat. With only one out, they loaded the bases.

Matt's brow pleated in an almost comically worried expression. "Fletcher is up next, their power hitter," he commented.

Suddenly Hilary really didn't want the home team to lose. She wanted Matt's smile to return. She wanted them to leave the stadium together on a triumphant note. She wanted to hold on to the heady excitement she'd cultivated over the past eight innings.

"Strike him out, Randy!" she yelled at the pitcher.

Matt glanced over at her in surprise, and then she realized that was the first time she'd gotten carried away enough to bellow impotently at a man who couldn't possibly hear her.

A resounding crack snapped her attention back to the diamond. "Oh, no," she and Matt agonized together as the ball shot toward centerfield. Then, amazingly, a glove went up, the ball was caught, thrown, and the game was over.

The stadium shook. Hilary looked over and realized she and Matt had unconsciously clenched hands in the final, tense moments of the game, and he showed no signs of letting her go. His energy flowed into her, enveloped her, warmed her blood and made her feel completely, agonizingly alive. Baseball alone couldn't be responsible for the way she felt at this moment.

"Did you see that catch?" he asked, exuberantly grasping her other hand and holding both of them close to his chest. "What a play! That was incredible! That was...that was the most...Hilary, what's wrong? Did someone spill soda down your back or something?"

For some unknown reason, she was close to tears. If only he would get as excited about her as he did about a silly game. "Everything's f-fine," she managed to choke out.

"You don't look fine." He moved one hand up to feel her forehead in a gesture that had become second nature to him when she was ill. "Are you sure?"

When she nodded, his gesture of concern gradually transformed into a caress, his gentle fingers moving lightly over her hair and along her temple. Hilary realized he wasn't as unmoved by her nearness as she'd thought. Her blood surged as he cupped her cheek in his palm and drew closer.

Her breath came in small, sharp gasps. Their surroundings receded until she was aware only of Matt, his touch, the hint of passion in his dark eyes, his mouth just centimeters from hers . . .

"'Scuse me!" A half-drunk fan pushed past them, shattering the moment.

Matt's passionate gaze turned quickly to consternation. He pulled away from her as if she were a hot branding iron. "Come on, let's get out of here." He turned and they began making a tediously slow path toward the exit.

The pressing crowd made further conversation impossible, for which Hilary was grateful. There wasn't any word to describe or explain away what had just occurred, unless it was "madness."

She expected Matt to start the car immediately and drive off, to get as far as possible from the scene. But when they were seated, he leaned his forehead against the steering wheel, looking like despair personified. "I thought a baseball game would be a nice, safe place for us to get back on track," he murmured. "How wrong could I be."

"A little too much adrenaline was pumping through our veins, that's all," she commented, trying for a casual air she didn't feel. But she hated to see him so distraught. "It's not the end of the world."

"I almost kissed you," he said, refusing to meet her gaze.

"That's hardly a good reason to commit hara-kiri."

"I swore to you it wouldn't happen again. I'm not being fair to you."

"Do you hear me complaining?" she shot back.

"Dammit, Hilary, this can't keep happening." He turned to look at her then. "What are we going to do?"

"How about giving in?" she suggested. "You ought to be listening to those wonderfully earthy instincts of yours instead of always fighting them. And a kiss isn't going to hurt anyone."

"Hah! You think it's going to stop with a kiss?" he said as he started the Saab's engine. "And you leave my instincts out of this. If I want to rise above them, that's my business."

"Rise above them? I'm sure glad not everyone has your high ideals, or our species would die off."

She had a good point, Matt acknowledged silently as they waited in a line of cars headed for the parking lot exit. Wouldn't the two of them make a wild contribution to the gene pool?

Whoa, he warned himself. Let's take this one step at a time. First, was Hilary right? Was he wrong to deny his longing for her? Could he accept what she offered and remain in control? By God, maybe he could. The prospect sent a shot of excited anticipation through his body.

"Matt?" she said after a long silence. "Matt, you're not arguing."

"I guess I really don't want to argue with you, Hilary," he said, coming to a decision he should have reached yesterday. "Everything you've said is correct."

"It is? I mean, you agree with me?"

"Uh-huh."

"What does that mean, exactly?" she asked cautiously.

With his eyes on the traffic merging onto I-70, he reached for her hand and squeezed it tightly, suddenly afraid she would disappear from his life as quickly as she'd materialized. "It means I can't fight a tidal wave." He could hardly believe what he heard himself saying. He must be out of his mind.

Finally, he'd managed to silence Hilary. She didn't say a word for the duration of the drive home. When he'd parked the car in the driveway, he returned his radio to the glove compartment. He climbed out of the car and stretched, checked to make sure he had everything, then slammed the door and walked at a leisurely pace toward the pink house. Hilary walked beside him, still ominously silent.

"I need to check the greenhouse," he said when they were inside. "Wait for me, I'll be right back."

Hilary allowed herself a small thrill at those words. *Wait for me.* They sounded so deliciously intimate. She sat down at the top of the stairs, her every nerve ending vibrating with anticipation.

She hadn't expected to win the argument she'd started in the car. His sudden acquiescence had literally shocked her into silence. She was delighted—and also filled with apprehension. He'd been so adamant about not wanting to get involved with her. What had changed? And what sort of involvement did he have in mind?

For all her talk about giving in to instincts, she had no wish to rush with Matthew Burke. Whatever waited around the corner, she wanted to prolong it as long as possible. Chances were better than good that their shared delight would be transitory, and that one or both of them would get hurt in the end. She was willing to risk that. Apparently he was, too.

"Are all the hatches battened down for the night?" she asked Matt when he appeared at the bottom of the stairs. She hoped he didn't notice how her voice trembled.

"All secure." He climbed the stairs and sat down next to her, close but not touching. "Hilary..." He hesitated.

"Second thoughts?" she asked, scarcely breathing the words. Please, don't let it be that, she prayed.

"No," he answered without hesitation, stilling her pounding heart. He plunged ahead. "But I want you to understand from the beginning. I have serious doubts about how all this will turn out. I can't make any guarantees."

"No one can make guarantees, Matt," she said softly. "But we'll never know how it will turn out until we give it a try."

Apparently that was the response he needed to hear. He leaned closer to her, his eyes on her full lips. "That's all I wanted to say. I'm going to kiss you now, Hilary."

How like Matt to declare his plans before the fact, she thought dazedly as he claimed her mouth with his. Unlike that first, desperate kiss in the greenhouse, this one was slow, sweet as warm syrup and heavy as the scent of Grandma's roses. Matt had a taste all his own, Hilary thought as his tongue pushed playfully against hers, engaging her in a delightful battle. He wrapped her braid around his hand and gently guided her head back, changing the angle of their kiss, swamping her with a whole new set of sensations.

His other hand smoothed its way down her collar and across her breast, quickly, almost as if by accident, but something inside Hilary leapt at the instantaneous contact. She ached for more. She wanted his hands on her, inside her clothing. An image flashed in her mind of his mouth closing over her hardened nipple, and she shivered. She'd never known an ache so beautiful and so profound.

"Oh, Matt," she whispered when he gently broke the kiss and pulled her head against his shoulder. She wanted to ask for more, but forced herself to keep silent. After the disastrous path the evening had almost taken, she knew how incredibly lucky she was to be in his arms, and she didn't dare push that luck.

Matt felt liberated. What a difference it made to embark on a kiss with the full force of his will behind him. There was no guilt, no confusion, no regret, only this unbelievable sense of rightness. If a kiss could do all that, what would happen when they made love?

If they made love, he corrected himself. He was determined to take this thing one cautious step at a time. They were no more compatible tonight then they'd been this afternoon. No matter how optimistic Hilary was, he knew they were headed down a path strewn with land mines.

Chapter Five

Hilary stood back and admired the bouquet she'd just assembled. Not quite satisfied with her handiwork, she rotated the vase of roses a few degrees, then added two more blooms to the opulently crowded arrangement.

"There, perfect," she said aloud as she picked up the vase and walked into the entry hall, where she set it on a small table. Matt would see it first thing when he got home from Lawrence, where he'd gone this afternoon to hear the Secretary of Agriculture speak at the University of Kansas.

She spent a few moments just admiring the pale pink blooms. Grandma's roses had outdone themselves over the past two weeks, ever since the baseball game. Matt insisted they were blooming because of his special formula rose food. Hilary personally believed the bushes were displaying approval of the crazy, wonderful things developing between herself and Matt.

He would laugh if she ever voiced that opinion aloud. But sometimes, when they stood together and gazed appreciatively at the bushes, he would exchange a mysterious smile with her. Then she would wonder if he didn't secretly believe some mystical force was at work.

She gave her vase one final adjustment, then turned and left to see about getting herself arranged for this evening. Tonight was a celebration, of sorts. In the fourteen days since Matt's tentative decision to "give in to his instincts," he and Hilary hadn't had one serious disagreement. That was a small miracle.

True, she'd had to bite her tongue to control the urge to snap at him when he spent ten minutes rearranging the dishwasher to his satisfaction, and when he'd trimmed the once wild-looking privet hedge into perfect, identical cones. But because she fully intended to prove to him they were compatible, she found other ways to get minor antagonism out of her system and avoid arguments.

Instead of bringing up the morning hot-water problem, she'd begun taking her showers at night. And ever since the day she'd caught Matt refolding all of the sheets and towels—he obviously didn't like the way *she* folded them—she'd stopped doing all but her personal laundry. She'd even tolerated a dinner of liver and onions without a whimper, folding most of it into her napkin and then throwing it over the fence to the terrier next door. Then she'd snuck off to the deli when Matt was watching a baseball game.

Anytime she felt herself getting irritated, she remembered that he was putting forth quite an effort, too. He never said a word when she spilled dirt or fertilizer or peat moss in the greenhouse; he merely followed behind her with his broom. He hadn't tried to reorganize the kitchen in several days. He'd even ridden in her car once without suggesting she pull through the car wash.

Relationships take a lot of work, her grandmother had told her more than once. "You got that right, Grandma," she said aloud as she stepped into a steaming bath and let the floral-scented bubbles envelop her. But she knew her efforts were well worth the reward every time Matt held her in his arms, or kissed her, or breathed light endearments into her ear.

Just the memory of his thrilling touch caused her to quiver somewhere deep inside. Her skin tingled from head to toe. She slid deeper into the silky water and closed her eyes with a sigh of contentment. With no conscious effort on her part, the image of Matt materialized in her mind's eye. She saw him standing before her in nothing but a loincloth, strong and magnificent as a proud savage. In one hand, he gripped not a broom, but a primitive-looking spear.

With his other hand, he reached for her.

Hilary giggled at the audacity of her subconscious. Matt, a savage? Well, maybe, she conceded. She sensed something untamed in him whenever his passion surfaced. But it was a part of him that remained under rigid control. She looked forward to the day when he'd let go, give in fully to those wonderfully active hormones of his.

Let it be soon, she prayed. Her spontaneous fantasies were getting wilder every day.

From the beginning she had recognized and honored Matt's need for caution. She'd curbed her own impulsive nature and let him set the pace of their physical involvement. But she knew he wanted her. She saw it in his eyes every time he looked at her, felt it in the way he touched her. It was only a matter of time before that wanting overwhelmed both of them.

"Soon," she murmured hopefully as she stepped out of the tub.

When she came downstairs again, she was swathed in a strapless dress of shimmery silver silk, an impulse buy from Swanson's that she'd brought home almost a year ago and had never worn. She'd matched it with silvery stockings and pearl-gray leather pumps. Her hair was swept up in a sophisticated twist. A diamond drop necklace teased the valley between her breasts.

Now all she needed was her grandmother's diamond drop earrings, which matched the necklace. She knew right where they were, too. Hilary had put them, along with most of her grandmother's other jewelry, into a leather box and stuck it in the bottom of an antique trunk that served as a coffee table in the living room.

As she walked by the kitchen, the tempting scent of simmering tomato sauce and fresh oregano greeted her. She glanced at her watch, noting that her homemade lasagna would be ready in another fifteen minutes. Surely Matt would be back soon.

When she cleared the top of the trunk and opened it, she found the leather box right on top with the earrings inside. She quickly clipped on the drops and replaced the box. Just as she started to close the trunk lid, she saw something that intrigued her—her grandmother's photo albums.

Hilary hadn't set eyes on them in three years. She'd put them away because the photos served as painful reminders of her loss. But time had distanced her from her grief. As she flipped through the first few pages, she thought only of the love that had surrounded her growing-up years. There was a picture of her grandfather, holding her as a baby. He'd died shortly after that photo was taken, so she couldn't remember him at all.

There were several fuzzy black-and-white snaps of Hilary as a scrawny toddler, a cracked Polaroid of Iris McShane in a bathing cap and a dreadful-looking swimsuit, one of Grandma blowing out the candles on her sixtieth-birthday cake. Hilary's freckle-faced school photos were scattered on various pages.

Conspicuously absent were any likenesses of Hilary's father. According to her grandmother, a nineteen-year-old, pregnant Iris had torn up every photo of him after he'd left her six months into their fragile marriage.

To this day Hilary had no idea what he looked like. Her mother had studiously avoided mention of him, and Grandma had only hinted of his personality, saying, "He liked everything to be done a certain way. And try as she might, your poor ma just never mastered that 'certain way.'"

Hilary shivered, thinking of another man she knew who liked things a certain way. Of course, it was silly to compare Matt to her father, a man she'd never known. They probably weren't anything alike.

She continued to flip through the albums, remembering an old dog from her childhood, a best friend from adolescence, a soft peach-colored prom dress her grandmother had made from a vintage pattern.

When she ran across a whole page of pictures of the Spring Sunrise rose, she recalled Matt's interest in the flower. It was as spectacular as she remembered, she thought as she removed the photos from the album. She'd show them to Matt and see what he thought.

"Hilary? What's burning?"

Matt's home, she thought with delight. But a grimace followed on the heels of her smile as she sniffed the air, glanced at her watch, and groaned. *The lasagna.* She'd been looking at the silly photos for well over an hour, completely oblivious to everything.

She shoved the albums aside and raced into the kitchen. Matt was just removing the pan from the oven. It was charred brown on top and appeared to be hard as a brick.

"Our dinner?" he asked, frowning at the unappetizing mess as he set it on top of the stove.

"'Fraid so," she said with a sigh of disgust. "I got distracted and lost track of the time."

"Must have been some distraction. I don't suppose you thought of using a timer?" he asked, taking in the kitchen's disorder with a critical eye. But he softened his comment with the hint of a smile, the one he reserved for her most ridiculous blunders.

Damn, she'd meant to clean up this mess before Matt saw it. "I did use the oven timer. I just didn't happen to be in the room when it went off. Sorry, Matt, I really wanted this meal to be special." She gave a self-deprecating sigh. "So much for that."

"Why a special meal?" His almost-smile faded as he took in her dress, her hair. "Hilary, you're all dressed up."

Obligingly she twirled around, arms outstretched, so that the skirt of her dress flirted shamelessly around her knees. "So I am," she countered. "You looked so handsome in your suit when you left earlier, it made me wonder why we couldn't both be dressed up for a change, have a nice dinner, some wine...." Her hands fell to her side as the dress shimmied to a standstill. "Oh, well."

"Don't write off the evening yet," he said in an obvious effort to cheer her up. "Why don't I take you out to dinner? There's no use wasting all this glamour on just me."

Exasperating man! Why did he think she'd gotten all gussied up, if not just for him? She almost asked him that. "I thought you didn't like restaurants," she said instead.

He shrugged. "Depends on the restaurant. And the company," he added, his eyes roaming up and down her slender frame meaningfully. "You really do look beautiful, Hilary. Like moonlight."

Those were the prettiest words she'd ever heard, she decided as warmth suffused her face. "Thank you," she said in a hoarse whisper, wondering why her voice had suddenly deserted her. She cleared her throat and added brightly, "Where shall we go for dinner?" Eating in a crowded restaurant wasn't exactly the evening she'd planned. She'd had in mind something a bit more intimate.

"Bryant's Barbecue?" He grinned boyishly at her horrified expression. "Just kidding. How about the Crystal Peacock?"

Her eyes widened appreciatively. For the Peacock she'd suffer the crowd. "That's better. But we'll come back home for dessert. There's a raspberry cheesecake in the fridge, and I didn't burn it, either."

"Mmm, maybe we should skip dinner and get right to dessert."

"No dice." She waggled an admonishing finger at him. "You offered dinner and I'm accepting. Just let me run upstairs and find a suitable purse. I don't think my brown leather monstrosity would add a thing to my outfit."

Matt nodded in silent agreement as he watched her hoist the huge satchel that served as her everyday handbag and sashay out of the kitchen with it dangling off her shoulder. She kept promising to clean it out "one of these days," but so far, that day hadn't come.

Feeling a bit ragged from the hour-long drive home from Lawrence, he pulled a comb from his pocket and went into the entry hall to use the mirror there. He paused when he saw the roses. He hadn't noticed them before in his concern over the burning smell. The gleaming pink-tinged blooms were artfully arranged in a small crystal vase, and their heady, sweet fragrance swirled all around him. He could tell Hilary had taken a great deal of care in the design and placement of the flowers, and he smiled fondly.

He was amazed at how quickly the rosebushes had rallied. He'd given them devoted care, but even so, he hadn't expected such a dramatic transformation. If he didn't know better, he'd think the roses were . . . ah, but he did know better, he reminded himself, shaking his head as he wandered into the living room. He was starting to think like Hilary, and that scared him.

He sighed when he saw the clutter in the living room. For heaven's sake, he'd only been gone one afternoon. Couldn't she at least—he stopped himself before he could continue the uncharitable thought. Hilary had gone to a lot of trouble to please him, with the dinner and the flowers and all. There was no reason for him to get upset at a little mess. He'd held his tongue over these small transgressions for two weeks, and he'd continue to do so. This was her house, after all.

Reflexively he started to stack the photo albums, wondering where they'd come from and where he ought to put them. Then he saw the half-dozen photographs strewn over the coffee table, and all thoughts of straightening up fled. He picked up one of the photographs and studied it intently. This had to be the rose Hilary's grandmother had developed. What had she called it? "Spring Sunrise," that was it.

He couldn't think of a more appropriate name. The fist-sized blossom was an explosion of fiery orange surrounded by pale yellow. Even in the faded colors of an old photograph, the flower was magnificent. No wonder it had won a prize. He'd love to see the real thing.

"Oh, there you are."

Matt looked up to see Hilary standing framed in the doorway and clutching a tiny silver evening bag. He was struck again by the moonlike shimmer that seemed to surround her.

"I see you found the pictures," she said as she glided into the room. "I ran across those and couldn't resist reminiscing. Of course all the while, I was letting the lasagna burn." As she spoke she hastily cleared off the top of the trunk and began shoving the photo albums inside. "So what do you think?"

"Magnificent," he murmured, his eyes on Hilary.

She blushed the way only she could. "I meant, what do you think of the Spring Sunrise?"

He struggled to return his attention to the photographs. "From what I can see in the pictures, it appears to be an extraordinary-looking specimen—maybe a once-in-a-lifetime occurrence. You know, the odds of producing an outstanding new rose from any one cross-pollinization are literally thousands-to-one."

"Really? Are you saying the Sunrise might be valuable?"

Matt shrugged, trying not to get too excited about a shot in the dark. "If the rose is reproducible. If it's hardy. If it's pest-resistant . . . there are a lot of 'ifs.' A new rose has to go through years of testing by a commercial rose breeder before it can be introduced to the public. Only about one out of a hundred new varieties taken on by the breeders is deemed good enough for introduction."

"Yikes, no wonder Grandma didn't want to go that route."

"You say she gave the rose away? Why didn't she give it to you?"

"Oh, she offered it to me. But it was a fragile plant, if I remember correctly, so I suggested she give it to one of her garden club friends, someone who knew what they were doing."

"But you don't remember who she gave it to?" he persisted. "I'd like to know what happened to it. It would be a shame if it were growing in a backyard somewhere, wasting away in obscurity when it could be very valuable."

She shook her head. "My memory is pretty fuzzy when it comes to that period in my life. Grandma was getting weaker every day, and it was all I could do to simply cope with that. She was my only family, and it was hard to accept that I was going to lose her."

Matt swallowed uncomfortably at her pensive expression. He hadn't meant to remind Hilary of something so sad, and now that he'd done it, he couldn't find anything appropriate to say. He'd never lost anyone close to him. His whole family was disgustingly healthy, including both sets of grandparents.

"I..." he started. "Never mind. It's probably not something we should pursue."

She looked at him with a surprised expression. "Why not?"

"Not if it's going to make you sad," he said firmly.

She looked even more surprised. "I'm not sad, really. In fact, just today I realized that the pictures in those albums don't give me even a painful twinge anymore. I was just trying to think who Grandma might have given that rose to."

THE
BIG
WIN

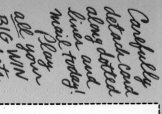

"Maybe one of her friends would know," he suggested, relieved that he hadn't upset her. "Are you still in touch with any of them?"

Hilary shook her head, lips pursed and brows drawn together in thought. Then her face brightened. "I have her address book somewhere. In a box in my closet, maybe. Want to help me look for it?"

He was already pushing himself off the sofa. Hilary turned and whisked her way out of the room and up the stairs, with Matt right behind. The mess in the living room was forgotten. So was dinner.

Two hours later they were sitting on the floor in Hilary's bedroom, the elusive address book still missing. Hilary had pulled at least half a dozen aging cardboard crates from the top of her closet and had systematically emptied them, stopping every now and again to remark over some item of memorabilia—a purple ostrich feather from an old hat, a packet of yellowed letters Hilary had sent to her grandmother from summer camp, a box containing a small collection of campaign buttons.

"But no address book," Matt commented, gazing at the array of papers and other odds and ends strewn all over the floor. An hour ago he'd given up trying to maintain any sort of order—Hilary had emptied the boxes with a speed that far exceeded his pace at packing them up again.

"Wait—oh, this is perfect!" she exclaimed, triumphantly holding up a tattered piece of paper.

Matt leaned closer to her to have a look. She held the 1975 Heart of America Garden Club Roster. "Do you think any of those numbers will still be good?" he asked.

"If we're lucky," she replied with undying optimism. "I just hope some of these ladies are still alive. The one time I went with Grandma to a meeting, everyone there had blue hair. Do you think it's too late in the evening to make phone calls?" she said, looking at her watch. Her eyes widened in shock. "Ten-fifteen? Good grief, we forgot all about dinner. I'm starving!"

Matt studied her briefly and tried to stifle his smile. The silver strapless gown looked somewhat ludicrous now, with her sitting cross-legged on the floor. Her sophisticated hairstyle was coming unglued, and several unruly red-gold curls had escaped to dangle impudently against her cheeks. She'd chewed off most of her lipstick. She didn't remind him so much of moonlight, now, but she was doubly adorable, rumpled and oh-so-touchable. He leaned closer, until he could catch a whiff of her airy fragrance, fading now. "Know what I'm thinking about?" he said in a low, husky voice.

"No, but I wish I did," she replied in kind, her words almost a whisper. "Tell me."

He almost did. "Raspberry cheesecake," he said instead.

Her smokey green eyes registered surprise, then laughter. "You're a terrible tease, Matthew Burke. And we can't have cheesecake for dinner... can we?"

"Who's going to tell us we can't?" he countered mischievously. He stood and pulled her up with him, letting one hand linger at her slim waist a little longer than necessary. He was hungry, and pigging out on cheesecake was perhaps decadent enough to distract him, although it wouldn't assuage the altogether different sort of hunger he felt for his delectable housemate.

She sighed. "I'm sure cheesecake is lacking in at least one of the four major food groups." Then she giggled. "But let's do it anyway. Let's be bold and reckless." She led the way downstairs, oblivious to how her innocent words taunted him. For once in his life he *did* want to be reckless. He wanted to ease that soft, silvery dress down to her waist and feel her softness against him. He wanted to kiss her in secret places until she moaned his name in ecstasy. He wanted to feel her long legs wrapped around his. He wanted... God, what didn't he want?

But something held him back—a subconscious warning of some kind, perhaps. The vast, unknown waters of this relationship instilled in him an almost unnatural caution, a compulsion to move ahead by only minuscule degrees, never biting off more than he could chew. To take this woman to bed at this stage would lend the relationship a certain seriousness he wasn't ready to commit to.

His rationale was almost superstitious, he realized. Nonetheless, as long as they didn't make love, he believed he could still back out gracefully, with his pride and his conscience intact.

The cheesecake was more than decadent, Matt declared when he took the first bite a few minutes later. It was sinfully sensuous. Unfortunately it did nothing to ameliorate his craving for Hilary. Listening to her soft sighs of delight and watching her supremely satisfied expression as she delicately nibbled the dessert only intensified his feelings. Dammit, *he* wanted to be the one to inspire that devilish sparkle in her eyes and the sated look on her face. Yet he was only fighting himself. He was fairly certain Hilary would welcome a deepening of their physical involvement. She hadn't pushed for it, but an unconscious invitation radiated from her eyes, even now.

He felt his heartbeat quickening. The temptation was almost too much. Almost. With his last ounce of willpower he stood, bid her a hasty goodnight, pecked her on the forehead and got out of there.

* * *

The next afternoon Hilary was still thinking about Matt's sudden departure from the dining room. He'd done that once before—when she'd served him French toast. Maybe her cooking had a peculiar effect on him.

As she cleared a place at the kitchen table and prepared to make some phone calls, she acknowledged the real reason for his abrupt leave-taking. His need had been etched in every line of his face. His reluctance mystified her.

She shook her head to dispel the mental image, then dialed the first number on the garden club roster, Agatha Adams. It wouldn't do to dwell on Matt's motives. He would come to her when he was good and ready and not a moment sooner. To give in during a weak moment wasn't his style. He'd probably decide on a date that suited him and mark it on his calendar.

"Hello?" a weak, squeaky voice greeted her.

"Hello, is Mrs. Adams there?"

"This is Mrs. Adams. Who is this?"

"My name is Hilary McShane, and—"

"Helen who?"

"No, Hilary. Hilary McShane. I'm Eileen O'Leary's grand—"

"I don't know any McShanes. What are you trying to sell?"

"Nothing. I'm Eileen O'Leary's—"

"Don't you try to fool me, young lady. You couldn't be Eileen O'Leary, she's passed on. Whatever you're selling I don't want." Click.

Hilary sighed and tried the next number. It was disconnected. No one answered the third, and with the fourth she got someone who'd never heard of Elizabeth D'arcy, the party she was trying to reach. At last, on the fifth try she reached a Mrs. Tom Durbin, who was lucid, had good hearing, and even went so far as to remember Hilary from the one time they'd met seven or eight years ago.

"How nice to hear from you, darling," the woman said graciously. "What can I do for you?"

"Do you remember a certain rose my grandmother developed, called the Spring Sunrise?" Hilary asked. "It was—"

"Oh, yes, that rose is almost legendary at the garden club. She won a regional prize for it, you know."

"Yes, I remember. Mrs. Durbin, she gave the rose away to someone before she died. I'm trying to track it down. You don't by any chance know who it was, do you?"

"No, dear, I surely don't. I have to confess, a lot of us were hoping she'd donate it to the garden club. We all wanted it—we were all just a little bit jealous, in fact. But I haven't heard a word breathed about it. If she did give it to one of the other ladies, it's a well-kept secret. I don't mind telling you, we were all dying to at least get a look at her notebooks."

"Notebooks?" Hilary repeated as her memory started to churn.

"Yes, you know. Those binders she kept her records in. Eileen was as scatterbrained as they come, except when it came to her roses. She recorded everything about every bloom she grew, *including* where they ultimately ended up, I'm quite sure. Find the notebooks and you'll find the Spring Sunrise."

"Notebooks," Hilary said once again, straining her brain to remember. "They were red. Yes, she had four or five red binders filled with notes she made on graph paper."

"That's right," said the older woman.

"Thank you so much, Mrs. Durbin." Hilary concluded the conversation quickly, then went to find Matt and tell him the good news. He was outside, raking up dried grass clippings and using them to mulch the tomatoes. She'd been helping him earlier, before lunch, but when there was just a little left to do, he'd dismissed her so she could make the phone calls.

She waved to him from the afternoon shade of the patio, holding up a glass of ice water enticingly. With a relieved expression he put down his rake and walked over to accept her offering. He took several large gulps of water, then held the glass to his perspiring forehead for a moment.

Hilary had felt her palms go sweaty from the moment she'd seen him, his gleaming, sweat-slicked muscles rippling in the sun as he toiled with the rake. He always got to her when he looked like this, hard and primitive and all male. Substitute a loincloth for his all-too-brief cutoffs, and he was last evening's fantasy savage come to life.

"I have some encouraging news," she managed to say in a normal tone of voice. She told him briefly about the phone call to Mrs. Durbin, gradually regaining her momentarily misplaced control. "I'm fairly certain I know where those notebooks are, too. I can see them in my mind's eye, sitting on a plywood shelf in a dimly lit place. They must be somewhere in the basement. Want to help me look?"

Chapter Six

The b-basement?" To his horror, Matt heard himself stutter. "You don't need to go down there. I can look for the notebooks..." But his feeble attempt to avoid a disaster went unheard. She'd already turned and was headed back inside, making a steady path toward the basement stairs. Resisting the urge to hide under the nearest rock, he followed, haunted by a premonition of impending doom.

"I can't believe I didn't think of the notebooks before," she chattered as she hopped down the stairs with a light step. "When it came to her roses, Grandma was almost compulsive about note-taking. She even drew pictures." Hilary reached the bottom of the stairs and pulled a string, switching on the light. She made a noise somewhere between a gasp and a strangled scream.

"Now, Hilary, it's not as bad as you think," Matt responded in a voice he might have used to calm an irritated grizzly bear.

She acted as if she hadn't heard. She made no further sound, merely swiveled her head slowly from left to right, her eyes wide and her mouth open. He tried to see it from her point of view: stacks and stacks of identical white cartons, lining the floor, lining the shelves, each neatly labeled to identify the contents. It did look pretty stark, especially with the new hundred-watt bulbs shining down from the ceiling. The only items not boxed were the ones too large to fit in the cartons: an exercise bike, a canoe, and a wicker chair badly in need of paint.

"What on earth did you do to my basement?" she finally said, sounding genuinely distressed.

"Cleaned it up?" he offered, remembering the room's chaotic state when he'd first arrived. He might have ignored the mess, except that he'd needed some elbow room. He'd started out just clearing some space on and around a workbench. But before he knew it, he'd filled dozens of cartons.

"You didn't clean it up, you sterilized it!" she cried. "How could you do this when you knew how I felt about—"

"No," he objected. "I did it while you were still in Alaska."

That didn't seem to make any difference to her. "This," she said, gesturing grandly with one hand, "is the work of an obsessive-compulsive. *No one* has a basement this clean. It even *smells* clean."

"It's a vast improvement," he stated firmly. "The way you had the junk piled up in here, I should have called an archaeologist in to excavate it."

"In the first place, it's not junk," she said, hands on hips and chin thrust forward defiantly. "In the second place, my filing system might have looked messy to you, but I knew where everything was. Now I'll never find anything."

"The cartons are labeled," he reminded her, suppressing the urge to laugh at her term "filing system."

"Oh, yeah? Tell me, in which of these cartons would I find the vintage dress patterns?"

Uh-oh, now she was putting him to the test. "That one," he replied with more certainty than he felt, pointing to a box marked "Sewing Supplies."

She was just dying to prove him wrong, Matt thought as he watched her pull the box off the shelf and open it. He was relieved to see that the yellowed patterns were indeed there, nestled among fabric remnants, spools of thread, thimbles and tape measures.

Hilary quietly closed the box and replaced it on the shelf. "What about my Christmas stocking?"

"If you keep naming off items, eventually you'll name one I can't find," he said through gritted teeth. "Try the one marked 'Christmas Decorations.'"

"All right, then, never mind the stocking. What about the notebooks?" she challenged. "There are four or five of them, red plastic binders."

Matt closed his eyes and tried to remember. But he couldn't recall running across anything like that, and he prided himself on his memory for details. "I don't think they're down here," he said earnestly. "I would remember something like that."

"Well *I* remember seeing them, and I'll find them if I have to open every box—"

"No, please, not that," he pleaded melodramatically. "I've seen the havoc you can wreak when you empty boxes."

She stared at him in astonishment for a few moments. "I'd laugh, except I know you're serious. It really would drive you crazy to see me mess the place up, wouldn't it? Basements are supposed to be messy."

"Not necessarily—"

"And greenhouses are supposed to be dirty. I mean, really, do you have to sweep the floor ten times a day? Next thing I know you'll be vacuuming up the dirt."

"I could tolerate the dirt if you'd just learn how to coil up a garden hose," he countered. "Honestly, every time you touch it, you leave it hopelessly snarled."

Hilary pushed up the sleeves of her sweatshirt, ready to jump in with both feet. "So if the snarls bother you, unsnarl the darn thing."

"I do, every day. Just like I pick up your tennis shoes off the living-room floor every day. And the wet towels you leave in the bathroom—"

"Speaking of the bathroom, have you ever timed your morning showers? Twenty-eight minutes on the dot!" She was shouting now. "Every single morning, twenty-eight minutes. Not only is that compulsively consistent, it uses up all the hot water!"

"You time my showers? Tell me *that's* not compulsive."

"And maybe I'd do a better job of cleaning up if you didn't follow me around and improve upon my efforts. I cleaned the glass door the other day. Five minutes later you were there with your handkerchief scrubbing away at some little spot I'd missed."

"I could have planted a garden in the spots you missed."

"Are you saying I'm a slob?" She stood on her tiptoes so that she was nose to nose with him.

"If the shoe fits—" Oh, hell. He'd gone too far. Her eyes blazed with fury and her hands bunched up into fists. He took two steps backward, not at all sure that she wouldn't take a swing at him.

"You're—you're—" she started to say, but she couldn't seem to form the words.

"I'm crazy is what I am," he said quietly as he turned and stalked up the stairs. He had to get away before any more caustic criticism could be hurled.

"And I *hate* liver and onions!" she shouted up the stairs at him, just before he slammed the door.

Hilary sat in the basement for a long time, taking deep breaths until she was calm again. Then, with her emotions carefully detached, she relived every ugly word she'd exchanged with Matt. All right, maybe she'd overreacted when she'd turned on the lights, expecting to see her familiar mountains of accumulated clutter. When instead she'd laid eyes on all these rows of identical boxes, she thought she'd entered another dimension.

She'd blown up. There was no other word for it. All of the small annoyances she'd suppressed for the past two weeks had roiled and burbled and surfaced all at once, beyond her control. She'd attacked.

Of course, Matt had obviously been doing a little suppressing of his own. It hadn't taken much to provoke him. And he'd called her a slob—or at least, he'd agreed when she'd called herself one.

Was this the end of their noble experiment, then? Had Matt been right all along? Were they just too different to peacefully coexist?

She'd have to think about it. If she knew Matt at all, he'd think about it, too. He'd brood while he puttered with the tomatoes and the roses, and he'd come up with the ultimate solution. And he'd arrive at it so logically that she'd be bound to agree.

It would be better if she could come to her own conclusion first and be prepared to defend it, she decided. She'd simply have to avoid Matt until she'd decided what it was she wanted from him—what she wanted for herself.

She crept up the stairs and peeked out the door. She didn't see or hear him. A moment later she looked out into the driveway and saw that his car was gone. Taking advantage of his absence, she quickly cleaned up the kitchen—*guilty conscience, Hilary?*—and went into her studio, closing the door behind her. She needed a few more paintings for the Plaza Art Fair in September, and there was nothing like an agitated emotional state to get her creative juices flowing.

She painted like a woman possessed, losing herself in color and form, letting her feelings guide her brush. By the time she came up for air, sunlight slanted through the windows at an alarmingly severe angle. She glanced at her watch and jumped in surprise—seven-thirty. She'd been painting for almost six hours straight. She set her paintbrush down and slid off her stool, stretching her protesting muscles. She forced herself to look at something else besides her work. But the sight of the backyard out the window only depressed her. She'd come to think of it as *their* yard, and *their* garden.

"That was a premature notion," she murmured.

When she returned her attention to her painting, she could hardly feel cheered. The canvas she'd agonized over for six hours was a likeness of Matt, dressed in his gardening uniform of cutoffs and T-shirt, bent over one of his tomato plants as if willing it to grow. She'd seen him do that more than once—stare at some growing thing as if silently communicating with it. She didn't imagine he was aware of the habit.

Once when he'd assumed that pose, she'd managed to whip out her sketch pad and quickly record the major lines of his body. At other times she'd surreptitiously drawn the musculature of his back, his capable hands, his legs, the texture of his windblown hair. From these drawings she'd created the painting that now sat on her easel.

It wasn't exactly right, she decided. She hadn't quite captured the correct facial expression. The features were Matt's, but the right emotions weren't coming through.

She sighed, unclamped the canvas from the easel and set it behind four or five other unfinished works she'd left leaning against a wall. She'd give it a rest and try again another day. She certainly was in no hurry to finish it, because she didn't intend to sell it at the Art Fair. This was one painting she'd keep in her personal collection, even if to look at it caused her pain.

Still keeping a wary eye out for Matt, she sneaked into the kitchen to grab something to eat. She popped a frozen diet entrée into the microwave, then peeled an orange while she waited. With a handful of peelings, she opened the cabinet under the sink, where the trash can was kept. She could hardly believe her eyes.

Sitting on top of the trash was an empty fast-food bag. Matt was definitely upset—he never, but *never*, touched fast food. She didn't know whether to feel triumphant or defeated over his agitated emotional state, but at least she knew she wasn't suffering alone.

She went to bed early, thinking that as taxing as the day had been she'd drop right off. But she dozed fitfully, plagued by vague, disturbing dreams. When she awoke with a start for what seemed like the fiftieth time, she turned over onto her back and sighed. The covers were twisted around her bare legs and her pillows had been tossed to the floor, testimony to her restless attempts to gain a sleeping state. She glared at the glowing digital display on her clock radio. Two a.m. and she didn't feel the least bit like closing her eyes.

The bedroom was hot and stuffy. She'd opened the windows before lying down, but the air outside was so still that not a breath of breeze stirred the gauze curtains. She'd go downstairs and get a fan out of the basement—if Matt hadn't boxed them up, that is.

Once she was downstairs, however, she forgot about the fan. The closed door to her studio drew her like a magnet. The unfinished painting called to her.

"I might as well," she grumbled, reaching for the doorknob. She opened the door and took a half-step into the room, then gave a small gasp of surprise. Matt reclined on the sofa in nothing but a pair of gym shorts, illuminated only by the television's glow.

"Excuse me," she said automatically as she started to retreat, feeling a bit disoriented by the unexpected sight.

"No, wait, it's okay," he said, sitting up and swinging his bare feet onto the floor. "What are you doing up in the middle of the night? Is everything okay?"

She stood halfway in, halfway out of the room, poised for flight. "Everything's fine. I just couldn't sleep and I thought I might do some painting, put my nervous energy to good use." She stepped closer to the TV screen. "Baseball? At two in the morning?"

"It's a videotape. I record the away games and watch them when I have time." He grinned sheepishly. "I know, you think it's compulsive."

Hilary felt slimy, hearing her derogatory label tossed back at her. "Not compulsive. A tad fanatical, perhaps..." He didn't smile. "Well, uh, you were here first. I'll go have insomnia some place else."

Matt turned off the television with his remote control. "That's okay. I can do this anytime. I don't want to stifle your creativity."

"Oh, you won't stifle it." Just his presence would probably feed it, but she didn't need to tell him that. "Go ahead and do what you were doing. I'll try not to bother you."

She busied herself setting up her easel and spreading daubs of paint on a disposable palette. Matt settled back down to watch baseball. But she sensed that not all of his attention was on the game. She felt suddenly vulnerable in her skimpy, red cotton nightshirt, which she'd been too hot to cover with a robe.

She turned on a small lamp and aimed it for her canvas, rather than using the overhead light. The television glow illuminated Matt's face perfectly. His expression of concentration was just what she needed to see in order to fix the painting.

They sat that way for almost an hour, silent. When the game finally ended with the Royals on the losing end of the stick, Matt ejected the tape and sat up to stretch and yawn. *Oh, don't move now,* she pleaded silently. She just needed him to model a few more minutes, but she was much too embarrassed to tell him what she was doing.

"I'm going to get a glass of water," he announced. "Would you like something?"

"Water would be nice. It's awfully hot. Sorry there's no air conditioning."

"I saw some fans in the basement. You want me to bring a couple up, for the bedrooms?"

Her mouth went even dryer at the mention of the basement. She and Matt had been polite, nicely skirting the issue that had divided them. Now it was suddenly out in the open. "Are they in the box marked 'Fans'?" she said with a mischievous grin, trying for humor.

She fell a little short of the mark. Matt didn't come close to returning her smile. He stared down at his bare feet.

"I wasn't trying to be spiteful," she said quickly. "I'm sorry I lost my temper about the basement. I'll get used to the boxes—as long as you don't mind if I give you a call once in a while so you can tell me where you put something."

"Once in a while?" he said, looking up sharply.

She sighed hopelessly. "Oh, Matt, you were right all along, dammit. We are irrevocably incompatible. You're neat, I'm messy, neither of us is likely to change, and we're driving each other crazy."

"Yeah," he agreed. "Are you saying it's over?"

She thought she detected relief in his voice. That helped her to strengthen the painful decision she'd just made. "We gave it the old college try, but . . ."

"At least we won't always wonder," he added. "You still want a glass of water?"

A painful lump in her throat prevented speech, so she shook her head.

"Well, then, good night."

So, this was the end, she thought as the door closed, blocking him from her sight, and tears filled her eyes. It seemed strange that something so important, something she and Matt had worked so hard on, should end with just a few empty sentences to note its passing.

She allowed herself to sob quietly, thinking the release might make her feel better. Moisture ran down her cheeks unchecked as she went through the automatic motions of cleaning her brushes, but the longer she cried the worse she felt.

She tried telling herself that this was all for the best in the long run, that if they hadn't ended things now they would only get into more hurtful arguments and never settle the differences that stood between them.

But could anything hurt more than this did?

Matt bolted upright in bed, not sure what had awakened him. It wasn't the heat this time; a front had moved through two days ago and brought with it a refreshing cool spell. He sat very still and listened, but all was dark and silent.

It was almost five o'clock—a little early to rise even for Matt, but he was wide awake so he decided he might as well get up. He'd get an early start on the watering, and maybe give the thirsty ground a chance to absorb some of the moisture before the greedy sun dried everything up. He pulled on an old, blue-striped polo shirt and a pair of jeans that were faded almost white, slid his sockless feet into beat-up tennis shoes, and headed downstairs.

He paused when he passed Hilary's door, and something inside him lurched as it did every time the thought of her took him unaware.

Two nights ago, when they'd agreed to call it quits, he'd stood outside her studio door for a few moments after he'd left her, and he'd heard her crying. It had been all he could do not to burst back into the room and take her in his arms, comfort her, tell her they'd work something out.

But one thing had stopped him. Could they ever make it work out? Or was theirs a doomed relationship, destined to be a ragged series of attempts and failures, more heartbreak, more tears? After several seconds of agonizing indecision, he'd forced himself to walk away from the sound of her crying. That was one of the hardest things he'd ever done.

The past two days had resembled the Cold War. Hilary continued to assist him with his work, carrying out her duties with uncharacteristic efficiency as if she couldn't wait to get done and get away from him. They'd spoken politely to one another but only when necessary. They'd seen to their own meals and kept to their own activities. They hadn't once come into physical contact, even innocently.

The Cold War was ten times worse than the silly argument they'd had, Matt decided as he moved past Hilary's door and down the stairs. He missed her smile and her easy laughter. He missed having dinner with her, sharing a pot of chili or cooking hamburgers on the gas grill. Hell, he even missed her damn tennis shoes in the living room. She'd assiduously avoided leaving them there these past couple of days.

The question was, what was he going to do about it, if anything?

He headed for the hall closet where he kept a flashlight. On the way he spotted the vase of roses in the entry hall, wilted and withered now, the heads of the blooms bowing sadly on their stems. Even as he gazed at them, a dried petal dropped to the shiny surface of the table.

Unable to bear the pitiful sight of them, he carried the vase into the kitchen, dumped the water, wrapped the dead flowers in a paper towel and thrust them into the trash. He wasn't sure if he was doing it for his benefit or Hilary's, but he didn't imagine she'd relish the sight of the dead flowers, either.

Outside, with flashlight in hand, he turned on the faucet to a moderate force and absently wandered over to the thriving roses. As he got closer, however, he realized something was dreadfully wrong. He set the hose down and stared in utter disbelief. Where were the blooms?

His first, irrational thought was that someone had stolen the flowers. But then he noticed that the blooms were there, they were just withered and shrunken to the point of almost disappearing. The buds that were opening were small, stunted things.

He examined each bush using the flashlight. No new buds were forming. The plants were having a relapse or something. He hadn't expected them to bloom indefinitely, of course, but it wasn't normal for blooms to die off so suddenly. Why would they, unless... unless they were displeased about the Cold War?

He groaned even as the thought formed in his head. Plants couldn't think, or feel, or respond emotionally, he reminded himself. Still, maybe it wouldn't hurt if he talked to them a little.

"Uh, hi, roses, how are you?" he said in a rusty voice, feeling utterly ridiculous. But he continued anyway. "I can see you're not feeling too well. But if you're refusing to bloom because Hilary and I had a fight, you can just cut it out. You aren't helping matters. I know how she feels about you guys, about what the blooms mean. If she sees you've stopped blooming, she'll take it as a sign that the relationship's really over, and I don't want her to believe that. *I* don't believe that."

As he said those words aloud, he realized it was true. He didn't believe for one minute that he would never hold her in his arms again, never kiss her. But something had to be done if he didn't want to lose her now, and he was the one who'd have to do it. He was the one who'd opened his big mouth in the beginning and declared them incompatible. Now it was his place to tell her he'd been wrong, that they owed it to themselves to try again, to try harder this time.

"All right, I'll call a peace conference," he told the roses. "We'll sign a treaty or something. Just don't stop blooming, at least not until I can get things straightened out."

Absently he touched one of the withering blooms, rolled it between his fingers. What were those bumps? He held the flashlight closer and peered at the flower. Ugh! Aphids! Abruptly he let go of the blossom and shook his hand to make sure none of the disgusting little creatures had clung to him.

"Aha, trying to fool me, were you?" he said to the bushes. "You're not blooming because you're infested! Well, I'll show you. I'll go to the garden center as soon as it opens and get some powder that will annihilate those aphids and—what am I doing? I'm talking to a rose-bush!"

He threw up his hands in disgust, picked up the forgotten hose, and put his mind to watering the garden. Hilary was driving him to do the strangest things.

Hilary drew back from the curtain at her bedroom window and stifled a giggle. She could not believe what her eyes had just seen—Matt, standing in the yard in the middle of the night, talking to a bunch of greenery.

The sound of his indistinct words floating through the window had awakened her. Wondering who he could be conversing with at this hour, she'd gone to the window to have a look. And there he'd been, standing before a rapt audience of rosebushes, carrying on an animated conversation complete with wild gestures and a lot of grimacing.

What in the heck had he been saying to them? she wondered as she drifted back to sleep. When she awoke a few hours later, the sun was shining brightly and a blue jay called shrilly outside her window.

"All right, all right, I'm getting up," she said irritably to the bird. She showered and dressed quickly, feeling like a slug for sleeping so late and anxious to get to work. Or was she merely anxious to see Matt, even though they were barely talking to one another? She'd made a great show of pretending indifference, but her heart still flip-flopped when she was within a hundred feet of him.

She sighed as she hurried downstairs. No matter that she and Matt had decided to end their relationship, she couldn't turn her feelings off as she would a faucet. She was still wild about the exasperating man.

All her hurry was for nothing. Matt wasn't even home, and he'd left her no instructions. So she lingered over a piece of toast with jelly and a cup of strong coffee, then wandered into the yard to see if any obvious chores needed doing. By now she'd learned exactly which tasks she could undertake on her own authority and which she had to okay with Matt.

But everything looked to be in order. The garden hose was coiled as neatly as if it had just been pulled new out of a package. She tested the soil in the various gardens, and all seemed appropriately damp. The tomatoes were showing their first tiny yellow blooms, she noticed. They were developing quickly, just as Matt had promised.

She turned her attention to Grandma's roses—and stopped cold. They were appallingly bare, with just a few, limp blooms clinging to the branches. "What happened?" she cried, coming closer to inspect them. "Oh, no, don't do this. You can't stop blooming, not now."

But they had, she conceded, just as abruptly as they had when her grandmother had died.

Was that why Matt had been talking to them this morning? Thinking back on the warm, fuzzy image she'd seen through her window, she acknowledged that it might have been only a wishful dream. It *must* have been a dream. Matt wouldn't talk to them. He thought that was a bunch of baloney.

She stood gazing at the barren bushes for a while longer, until she was struck with inspiration. It was a silly idea, really, but the more she thought about it the more appropriate it seemed. If the darn bushes were determined not to flower, then she'd have to take drastic action of her own.

She looked at her watch. The drugstore would be opening in ten minutes, and she'd be the first customer, she decided, returning to the house to get her purse.

It was late morning by the time Matt came back fortified with a five-pound bag of powdered insecticide. He tucked it under his arm and walked around the side of the house and into the backyard.

"Y'er dead meat, aphids," he declared as he plopped the bag onto the ground and ripped it open with a flourish. Not even bothering with gloves, he started to reach his bare hand into the bag when something in his peripheral vision stopped him. He paused, looked up at the bushes. "What the—where did those come from?"

At least a dozen, huge pink blooms nodded at him, all full and healthy, all—silk, he realized as he got a closer look. Someone had taped a bunch of silk roses to the—no, not someone, Hilary, he realized, taking a deep breath to steady himself. What a crazy thing to do. What a crazy, insane, *wonderful* thing to do. He wished he'd thought of it.

"Hilary!" he called out when he could trust his voice not to crack. "Hilary, I know you're around here somewhere!"

"I'm right here, you don't have to bellow," she answered, peeking out from behind the corner of the garage, where she'd been hiding and watching not five feet from him.

He crooked his finger toward her, suppressing his smile.

Cautiously she stepped away from her hiding place and approached. "Did you want something?" she asked innocently.

"Do you have anything to say about this?" he said, plucking one of the silk roses off the bush and holding it almost under her nose.

"Pretty, isn't it?" He brushed the petals lightly against her cheek. "Oh, my, it's made of silk." she said with mock surprise.

"Uh-huh. How do you explain that?"

"Uhhh, we have some talented silkworms living in our bushes?" she offered with a mischievous smile. But immediately she sobered. "Oh, Matt, I just couldn't stand seeing those bare bushes. It was like—" Her voice broke.

"Like what?" he urged gently.

"Like the roses had given up on us."

"If they gave up," Matt said cautiously, "maybe it was because we gave up—too soon."

Her face lit up with hope. "Do you really believe that?"

He hesitated. "About the roses giving up on us?" He made a tilting motion with his hand.

"No, I mean, do you believe we gave up too soon?"

"Yes," he answered, this time without hesitation. His hand moved to cup her cheek. "Hilary, I'm sorry about the basement. I swear I'll never do anything that drastic again."

She chuckled, running her fingers along the collar of his shirt. "There's not much left for you to organize, except the attic. Don't even think about it."

His flesh caught fire where she touched it. "Have you timed my shower lately?"

She frowned. "Oh, please, forget I said anything about—"

"No, I won't forget it. Why didn't you tell me before that I was using up all the hot water? We can't hold back things like that or we'll end up exploding like volcanoes again." He ran his fingers along her hairline. "I'm down to seventeen minutes in the shower, and that includes a shave. Not bad, huh?"

"But I said so many hateful things—"

"Things you should have brought up a long time ago. You told me you *liked* liver and onions."

"I wanted to prove we were compatible," she explained somewhat miserably.

"We aren't compatible," he said, pulling her closer. "So we'll just have to work around that fact, won't we." His lips closed over hers, giving her no more opportunities to argue.

God, she tasted sweet, he thought dazedly. She smelled great. She felt even better, all warm, soft, inviting curves that somehow aligned perfectly against his own body. How could he have let her go so easily? How could he have been so foolish as to let a silly argument tear them apart?

"I told you at the beginning this wouldn't be easy," he murmured against her hair somewhere near the vicinity of her ear.

"Nothing worth having comes easily," she whispered back, her breath tickling his ear. "My grandmother used to tell me that all the time."

"Does that mean you'll try again?" he asked.

She nodded. "I might even learn how to coil a garden hose."

Chapter Seven

Matt!" Hilary called out as she staggered through the front door one July morning, loaded down by two heavy sacks of groceries. "Help, Matt, where are you?" she called again as one of the sacks slipped precariously.

No answer.

Where had he gotten to? she wondered as she crab-walked awkwardly into the kitchen with one sack sliding down her thigh. She managed to make it to the table, however, without dropping anything.

She hoped Matt hadn't forgotten about the block party. Then she read the note on the refrigerator and realized that not only did he remember the party, but he was planning to cook something grand for the all-day potluck feast. In the note he politely requested that Hilary "stay out of the kitchen so as not to disturb the brilliant chef."

"Stay out of my own kitchen?" she argued aloud to the empty room. "Not on your life, buster." Not when she had her world-famous mulberry-lemon pie to prepare. She opened the refrigerator and found it full—literally full, so that not one cubic inch of space was left to receive her newly purchased groceries. What in the world was all this stuff? She felt as if she were staring at an ad for a supermarket sweepstakes.

She decided not to worry about cooling down her perishables until she'd gotten the pie started. But a cursory search in the fridge for the crust she'd made last night proved fruitless. She began removing plastic containers at random, hoping to uncover the crust. When at last she found it, pushed to the very back, it was cracked down the middle.

I'm not going to get mad, she told herself sternly. What she didn't need today was another screaming match with Matt. They'd already quarreled once today, over something stupid—ah, yes, the arrangements of gardening tools. As if they needed to be arranged at all, for heaven's sake!

Matt's suggestion that they bring up grievances as they arose instead of holding everything inside had seemed valid at the time. But for the past month or so they'd been "clearing the air" on at least a daily basis—and arguing like a couple of noisy blue jays.

Of course, after they had a fight they got to make up, Hilary mused as a warm rush of longing invaded her senses. Their breathless reconciliations almost made the fighting worthwhile. Almost.

"Hilary, what are you doing?"

She jumped at Matt's sharp question, then steeled herself to answer civilly. "Repairing the piecrust that *you* smashed."

"What piecrust?" he asked as he set a small basket of garden-ripe tomatoes—their first crop—onto the table.

"I'm sure you didn't notice it. That's why you smashed it."

"Oh. Sorry. What are you doing in here, anyway? Didn't you see my note?"

"Sure did. But you aren't chasing me out of my own kitchen. I have things to do."

"Well, I suppose we can share counter space. Just as long as you don't need the oven."

"Of course I need the oven!" She caught her voice rising and quickly checked it. "I'm making a pie," she continued in a more normal tone. "A seven-year-tradition pie."

Matt checked his watch. "I'll be done at about eleven. Can you wait till—why is that stuff sitting out?" He was staring at the plastic containers on the counter.

"Oh, just some stuff I took out of the fridge when I was trying to find the piecrust."

"That's not just stuff, those are the ingredients for my recipe. And they need to be cold," he added huffily, replacing the containers and rearranging items in the refrigerator until everything was perfectly aligned.

"If you keep standing there with the door open, nothing's going to be cold."

"If you'd put the stuff back in the first place—" He cut himself off with an obvious struggle to master his temper.

Hilary knew that if she stayed there any longer the argument would only escalate. And she didn't trust herself not to grab one of those lovely, ripe tomatoes and pitch it at him.

She began to pack her pie ingredients into an empty grocery sack. "You can have the oven as long as you want. I'll make other arrangements."

"C'mon, Hilary, don't leave mad. You can use the oven first."

"I'd rather leave mad than argue," she said as she made a rushed exit.

She headed for Sheila's house. Her neighbor was planning a watermelon boat of fruit salad for the party, so she wouldn't be needing her oven.

Sheila accepted Hilary's presence without question for a few minutes, allowing her to vent her frustration in peace by banging around her pots and bowls, and stirring her pie filling as if she were trying to beat it to death.

But finally Sheila broke the silence. "Dare I ask why you're not at home doing this?" she asked as Hilary set the patched crust into the oven.

"Matt commandeered my kitchen. He's preparing something large and secret, and being terribly haughty about the whole thing."

"I don't get it," Sheila said as she plucked a red grape off its stem and dropped it into an intricately carved boat of watermelon rind. "Why didn't the two of you collaborate on something for the party? I know you both like to cook..." Her voice trailed off at Hilary's unabashed laughter.

"We've never tried to cook together. This morning I found out why. We'd kill each other."

Sheila dropped the last of the grapes into the boat and threw the empty stem into the trash. "Are you going to tell me what's going on between you and Matt, or do I have to drag it out of you?" she asked point-blank. "You two have been living in that house together for a while now and I haven't heard a peep out of either one of you regarding the true state of affairs. All I get are these intriguing, cryptic remarks."

"What are you expecting to hear?" Hilary asked innocently.

"By now I thought you'd be naming your children."

"Sheila! Since when did you start matchmaking?"

"I'm not. At least, I didn't start out with matchmaking in mind," she corrected herself. "When I asked Matt to take Meredith's place, I had no idea you'd be coming home from Alaska early. But that first day I saw the two of you together..."

"What?"

"Sparks. And don't try to tell me they weren't there. You were sick but you weren't in a coma. At the time I wondered why I hadn't introduced the two of you before."

"I know why," said Hilary with a sage nod of her head. "We're totally incompatible."

"Oh. Then there's...nothing?" Sheila looked so crestfallen that Hilary felt compelled to cheer her up.

"Not nothing, exactly. Something. I'm just not sure what."

Sheila immediately brightened. "I just knew it. I'm never wrong about these things. Tell me everything, and don't leave out a single detail." She pulled her chair closer to the table and pushed the watermelon boat aside. "I brought the two of you together, so I have a right to know."

Though Hilary pretended reluctance, she was dying to confide in someone. She'd never been inclined to gossip about her love life. But since she was somewhat befuddled by the twists and turns of her relationship with Matt, perhaps a second opinion was in order—especially from Sheila, who had known Matt all his life.

So as she worked on the filling for her pie, she explained about the baseball game and the tentative decision they'd reached that night. And the cautious two weeks afterward, during which they'd pretended a harmony that didn't quite exist...the blowup in the basement...the miserable two days Matt referred to as "the Cold War"...the peace treaty, sealed with that searing kiss among the counterfeit roses.

"This major reconciliation happened when?" Sheila asked.

"A month or so ago."

"And how have things been going since then?"

"In fits and starts. Half the time my head is in the clouds, and I don't care how different we are. I push logic aside and I'm supremely happy."

"And the other half of the time?" Sheila raised one inquiring eyebrow.

Hilary sighed. "He still drives me crazy. I'm walking on eggshells trying so hard not to displease him, and yet I always manage to. And boy, do I hear about it."

Sheila poked at the watermelon boat with a toothpick. "That doesn't sound like Matt. I've always thought of him as so diplomatic."

"We tried diplomacy," Hilary explained. "Now we're going with brutal honesty."

"And?"

"We spend a lot of time arguing."

"Well, that's not so bad. Every couple argues."

"We don't just argue. We scream like banshees. The neighbors can probably hear us up and down the street."

"Hmm." Sheila pursed her lips and went to work on a cantaloupe. "Are you compatible in...other areas?" she asked cautiously.

Hilary couldn't fail to guess her meaning. "I imagine we would be," she answered. "I don't actually know."

Sheila turned as red as the watermelon. "Oh. I just assumed, living in the same house and all..."

"It's okay, Sheila," Hilary said soothingly. "I know it seems odd in this liberated day and age, but we're taking things slowly." As a snail, she added silently.

"Hmm." Sheila said again, absently rearranging the grapes, strawberries and melon balls. She stuck colored toothpicks into the fruit until the boat resembled a rainbow porcupine. "This doesn't look much like the viking ship in the picture, Hilary. You're the artistic one, you give it a try."

Hilary was glad to oblige. She started removing the toothpicks, rearranging the fruit into a colorful pattern as she went. "So what do you think about Matt and me?" she prodded when Sheila offered no opinion.

"I think you need a new approach, if brutal honesty isn't working."

"I just don't know what else to try," said Hilary, returning her attention to the pie filling. "Matt and I have already agreed that we are the way we are, and we can't change."

"Of course you can change. Don't fall for that old saying, 'You can't teach an old dog new tricks.'"

"I don't know," Hilary said, taking her browned pie crust out of the oven. "We've tried to reform each other. It hasn't worked in the long run. Maybe we're just not committed enough to the relationship." She hated to admit that out loud, but she was afraid it was true. In the weeks they'd been together, neither of them had even once mentioned the future.

"Maybe if you got some of this stuff worked out, commitment would follow," Sheila suggested practically. "Commitment, engagement, marriage..."

"We're not getting married," Hilary said firmly. "You know that I don't intend to marry at all, much less a perfectionist like Matt."

"Then what's the point of working out the differences?" Sheila asked with seeming disinterest, as if she'd tired of the subject. "Why not just scratch and kiss for the rest of the summer? Then it'll all be over. Hey, and I have this cousin I could introduce you to. He's unbelievably messy. The two of you would get along like pigs in slop. There, how does the boat look now?"

"Terrific," she responded halfheartedly, her mind still on Sheila's previous comment. She didn't want to meet some slob of a cousin. She wanted to work things out with Matt. But was there a point? Why was it so important they get along when in another month or so he'd be moving out of her house, and probably out of her life?

"Hey Mom, hurry up! You said you'd enter the sack race relay—oh, hi, Hilary." Bryan skidded to a halt at the kitchen door.

"Hi, Bry," Hilary greeted him cheerfully, trying to dispel her dismal thoughts.

"We'll be right there, Son," said Sheila. "You tell them not to start without us."

Hilary quickly poured her pie filling into the crust and popped it into the oven. Then she lugged the watermelon boat outside while Sheila grabbed paper napkins, cups and a pitcher full of tropical punch. As they made their way to the tables where numerous other food offerings were displayed, Hilary could see that festivities were already well underway.

The block party had been an annual event on Jenny Street since Hilary could remember. Barricades had been erected on either end of the block to keep the traffic out. Teenagers were skateboarding at one end of the block.

Toddlers were running around table legs and chairs at this end, chasing dogs and runaway cups of juice and each other with total abandon. Bob, in his appointed role of Master of Ceremonies, was trying to organize a half-dozen older children and their parents into a sack race. Several other silly contests were scheduled throughout the day. A disc jockey would come in the evening with some dance music. And, of course, there would be nonstop gorging on homemade goodies of every variety.

Hilary was curious how Matt would survive his first Jenny Street block party. The residents always welcomed newcomers, but she had to wonder how well he'd fit in. The party was loosely organized at best and wildly chaotic at worst. It might be enough to send him into hibernation.

"I'll see you later, Hilary," said Sheila when everything was arranged on the table to her satisfaction. "I'm being summoned to the sack race."

Hilary waved, but she was already scanning the crowded street for Matt. They still had a disagreement to resolve, and the sooner she found him, the sooner they could make amends and maybe enjoy a carefree day together. When she didn't locate him, she decided to wander back to the house and see if she could scare him up.

When she opened the front door, she almost ran right into him. He was carrying a huge... thing of some sort.

"Yikes, you scared me. What *is* that?" she asked, eyeing the peculiar food dish with awe. At least, she assumed it was food. It looked like some sort of exotic cactus, or a giant, multicolored pinecone.

"It's a nacho tree," Matt answered, beaming like a proud father over a precocious child.

"Yes, I can see that now," she responded skeptically as she realized the pointed objects sticking out all over the thing were tortilla chips. *Blue* tortilla chips. They were stuck in a fat, cone-shaped mountain of layered beans, cheese, guacamole and who could tell what else.

"What did you do, sculpt the thing?" she asked, staring at the striped wonder.

"Yup. And I'll kindly request that you reserve judgment until you taste it."

"Oh, okay, since you asked." She started to reach for a chip.

He snatched the object out of her reach. "Not yet. At least let everyone get a look at it in its full glory first."

She rolled her eyes as she held the door open for him to exit. She followed him to the food tables, appreciatively taking in his nicely muscled, tanned legs encased in gleaming white tennis shorts, topped off by a strawberry-red knit shirt. *Delicious,* she caught herself thinking. She'd rather have a taste of him than his darned old nacho tree any day. But first they'd have to make up.

An apology was in order, she supposed. She'd been awfully grumpy this morning. But the prospect didn't much appeal to her.

Matt set the "thing" down by the watermelon boat to a chorus of *oohs* and *ahs*.

"It's almost too pretty to eat, Matt," Meredith called out from where she sat in the shade of a huge pecan tree, her wrapped knee propped up on a stool. At least two young men were paying her court, waiting on her hand and foot.

"Not bad, Matt," said Sheila, who leaned over to inspect the tree at close range. Threads of burlap from the recent sack race clung to her legs. "Whatever it is, it looks great, and I need some sustenance." She reached for it.

"Wait." Matt held up his hand to ward her off, hesitated, then said, "Nah, never mind, go ahead."

Sheila looked up, poised to grasp. "Is there a problem?"

Hilary stepped in. "I think Matt wants us to admire it awhile longer before you dig in. After all, he did work *all morning* on it. Hours and hours in the kitchen, monopolizing every square inch of counter space—"

"Er, Hilary," Matt interrupted as her voice grew more shrill. Just then a Frisbee whooshed past them and sailed right into the nacho tree, decapitating it.

Hilary couldn't help herself. She laughed at the disastrous results. All Matt's hard work reduced to a huge, formless glob.

"Get a grip," Sheila whispered sternly, then smiled apologetically at Matt.

"Well, so much for admiring," Matt said with a grin and a shrug. "Dig in, Aunt Sheila." He grabbed a chip slathered with guacamole and popped it into his mouth. Then he turned to Hilary. "You, come with me."

"But—"

"Now." He clamped an arm around her waist and led her through the throng, smiling and waving to several of their neighbors. She had no choice but to go with him, although she would have anyway. She recognized the tautness around his mouth and the stiffness of his body that hinted at the anger he held just below the surface. And no wonder he was mad. What had possessed her to belittle him and his masterpiece, anyway?

He found a grassy spot under a tree in someone's yard, far away from the center of activity. He sat down, pulling her down beside him none too gently. "Now just what the hell was that all about? If you're really angry about the piecrust, then by all means let's talk about it. But I draw the line at public bickering."

"I didn't do it on purpose," she answered, looking anywhere but at Matt. "It just slipped out."

"What are you so ticked off about? Hilary, I've tried not to make waves. I've tried to be considerate. But no matter how I try, we end up arguing over the stupidest things."

"I don't know why I'm so angry," she answered miserably. "These past few weeks I've felt restless and edgy all the time. Deep down I know you weren't hogging the kitchen on purpose, and I'm sure the piecrust was an oversight. But for a moment I honestly believed you'd purposely sabotaged me. And I wanted to see that nacho-tree thing down the front of your shirt." She sighed. "I'm sorry, Matt. I really am this time."

He put his arms around her and pulled her against his shoulder, pressing his lips lightly to her temple. "I know you are, Hilary. I am, too."

They were quiet for a time. Matt absently caressed her arm with his forefinger. She snuggled closer to him despite the July heat.

Matt finally broke the silence with an unexpected chuckle. "The Frisbee in the nacho tree was pretty funny," he said.

Hilary stifled her own giggle. "I shouldn't have laughed, though. But I felt like steam was building up inside me and it just came out."

"Steam, you say?" He gave her a mischievous smile. "I know how we can let off some steam. Come with me?" It wasn't a command this time, but an uncertain request. She was happy to comply. Matt led her to the table where Bob was signing people up for various events. "What's next on the agenda?" he asked.

"Water-balloon toss, coming up in about ten minutes," Bob answered. "You and Hilary want to play?"

"Definitely."

Hilary looked at him uncertainly. But given his wicked grin, she could hardly demur.

Ten minutes later they stood facing each other along with seven other couples. Matt watched as Hilary was handed a bulging, pink water balloon. She gave him a steely look and patted the balloon menacingly.

"When I say go," Bob announced, "you ladies *gently* toss your balloons to the gentlemen. Then everybody takes a giant step backwards, and the men toss to the ladies. The last couple left with an unbroken balloon wins."

Matt had a strong feeling his partner didn't want to win.

"Ready, go!" Bob shouted.

Hilary cocked her arm and heaved the pink water bomb at Matt. Reflexively he ducked but wasn't fast enough. The balloon exploded against his chest.

"Oops, I guess we lost," she said sweetly, just before she turned tail and ran.

"Give me that!" he said, stealing a purple water bomb from the man standing next to him, then taking off after Hilary.

"This is highly unorthodox," he heard Bob saying behind him. Hilary was fast, but Matt was faster and his aim was good. He caught her right between the shoulder blades.

She stopped, water dripping from her hair, her shirt, her shorts. She turned, a fierce expression on her face. Then she exploded in laughter. "You said we should let off some steam," she said as she backed away from his relentless approach. But she let herself be caught. He pulled her to him, dipped her halfway to the ground and kissed her like Rhett kissed Scarlett. Their dramatic embrace was accompanied by loud applause and several disrespectful hoots.

Hilary threw her arms around his neck and kissed him back. She didn't care that the whole neighborhood was watching. She reveled in the feel of his lips on hers, his water-slick hands against the back of her neck, his fingers wound in her damp curls. "You are one sexy devil when you're out for revenge," she said with a low chuckle, running her hands over the front of his dripping shirt. She could feel his heart thumping wildly against her palm, echoing her own racing pulse.

"And you're one sexy lady when you're soaking wet," he said, staring pointedly below her neck. Her white blouse was all but transparent, and a lacy, plunge-front bra was outlined to perfection by the clinging white cotton.

"Oops. Looks like I ought to change clothes," she said.

"Not on my account, I hope." He lazily fingered the collar of her blouse, thinking he'd never seen a more arousing sight. It was all he could do not to unbutton the blouse right there in the middle of the street.

"For them, not for you," she said, glancing down the street toward their neighbors, most of whom had returned to their own business. "Unless you think I ought to go back to the party like this—"

"Not on your life," he growled. "Half the husbands on the block might be tempted to leave their wives if they saw you looking like that."

"And what are you tempted to do?" she asked coquettishly as they started walking toward the house.

"I'm tempted to slowly remove your clothes and make love to you." The impulsive words were out before he could even think about it, surprising him and shocking Hilary into silence. He'd never said anything like that to her before. From the onset of their relationship, he'd forced himself to go cautiously, never to say or do anything without thinking about it first.

It wasn't that he hadn't thought about making love with her. Hardly an hour went by that he didn't. But he'd promised himself that he wouldn't give in to that particular temptation unless the relationship began to head in a more serious direction. No matter how he desired her, taking her to bed casually just wasn't his style.

But now when he looked at her, for the first time a future with Hilary didn't seem hopelessly out of reach. Just the fact that they were both unwilling to let the relationship go, despite the tough time they were having, seemed to indicate a certain degree of commitment. Maybe that's why he'd said what he did.

"Are you propositioning me, sir?" she asked, leaning back against the front door with her arms folded. "Or was that just idle chatter?"

He seized her face between his palms and moved closer until he was eye to eye with her. "I was stating a fact. I'm tempted." He slowly released her, letting his fingertips trail over her cheeks.

She reached behind her to open the door, never pulling her gaze away from his. "I'm tempted, too," she said softly, her voice now devoid of any teasing. They stepped through the door, closed it and locked it behind them. She moistened her lips with a flick of her tongue. "I've been tempted a long time."

"So have I."

"But you never gave in to temptation before."

"I never felt quite like this before."

"Like what?"

Could he put it into words? She deserved to know why he suddenly wanted to make love to her. He was obliged to try to talk it out. "I feel like, for the first time there's something real and solid between us, something lasting."

"But we fight like alley cats," she objected, looking confused.

"And yet we don't give up. If I didn't believe in a future for us, I'd have thrown in the towel by now. Wouldn't you?"

She nodded, though somewhat uncertainly.

"I want to make love to you, Hilary. I want to make you mine—not just for now, not for a day or a week or—"

She grasped him by the shoulders and silenced him with a kiss. Her mind shut out the words. She didn't want to talk anymore. She didn't want to think. She just wanted to feel.

He responded to her mild aggression in kind, wrapping his arms around her possessively, returning her kiss with a heat that did seem to brand her as his. She moved her hands between them, running them over the length of his lean middle to the hem of his wet shirt. They pulled apart just long enough that she could peel the shirt over his head. Then she was back in his arms. His bare flesh felt cool from the wet shirt, but quickly warmed to her touch.

He planted tiny, hot kisses along her jaw and the sensitive column of her throat. His fingertips trembled along her collarbone, then came to the top button of her blouse. He disengaged it, and the next, then pushed the garment away from her neck and down, taking her bra straps with it.

He dipped his head to kiss the creamy flesh of her shoulders revealed by his actions. He kissed first one shoulder, then the other, paying them homage with teasing nips and kisses as light as a mist against her skin.

Hilary was swamped with feelings of the most indescribable kind. She was struck by Matt's sensitivity, the way that his every gesture was meant for her pleasure, to make her feel cherished. But she was also struck by something else, a dark thread of something wrong that wound its way through her consciousness like an insidious spiderweb, slowly choking her pleasure. Matt's words, which she'd tried to block out, came floating back to her now...*real*...*solid*...*lasting*... *future*...*mine not just for now, but for*...forever? Was that what he would have said if she hadn't cut him off?

Her mind reeled. He hadn't said the word, but she knew what was in the back of that neat, orderly mind of his. Forever...eternity...*marriage.* That's what had changed, why he'd suddenly thrown caution out the window. That was the only explanation that made sense. A wave of panic washed over her.

"No," she moaned as he fumbled with the next button on her blouse.

His hands stilled. "What?"

"We can't. I can't," she heard herself saying miserably. "I have to think."

"Hilary, what's wrong?" He pulled the shirt back over her shoulders. "I didn't think I was rushing."

"No, it's not that." To her consternation she felt tears welling up in her eyes.

"Then what?"

His words were so filled with concern, so tender, that more tears joined the first ones. "I just have to think, that's all." How could she explain her aversion to marriage? How could he know of the pain her mother had suffered, the inadequacy she'd felt when she'd failed to become the wife her husband had wanted? How could Matt understand how very much Hilary was like her mother when he'd never known Iris? How could he know that she'd tried once to adopt the mind-set of a wife and had failed?

She turned and ran up the stairs before he could see her crying—before he could stop her.

He stared at the empty space where she'd stood only moments before, warm and passionate and more than willing. What had happened? What had sent her running to her room like a flighty virgin?

She wasn't a virgin, he was pretty sure of that. Sheila, a wealth of unsolicited information, had told him all about Stephen, the jerk Hilary had almost married. The idiot had tried to pin her wings. No wonder she'd bolted.

Was that why she'd suddenly run away from him just now? Did she see him as another Stephen, eager to claim her as his own and mold her into some ideal he had of the perfect partner?

He wouldn't blame her if she did believe that. He'd done nothing but try to reform her from the night they'd met.

He'd behaved like an idiot! Instead of trying to change her behavior, he ought to work on his own, he mused with a sudden surge of inspiration. When in Rome...?

Chapter Eight

Hilary wandered down the stairs later that afternoon, dry-eyed and grim. After practically crying herself sick and then brooding for a couple of hours, she'd pulled herself together, repaired her makeup and hair, and changed her soggy, wrinkled outfit for a freshly ironed sundress. As she'd attended to these chores, she'd tried to view her situation from every angle. But no matter how she looked at it, the painful conclusion she'd reached was the same: She had to end things with Matt.

She should have seen this coming a long time ago, she berated herself as she filled the copper kettle with water and set it on the stove to heat. Matt was a man who tackled everything with single-minded, almost frightening intensity. Why would he approach a romantic involvement any less seriously? His own nature had made it difficult for him to get involved with her at all, she realized. The uncertainty had plagued him. It had gone against his grain to pursue something he didn't believe in one hundred percent.

That's why he'd held back from making love, too, because he equated that most intimate act with a commitment he hadn't been ready to make.

Apparently his feelings had altered somewhere along the line. He'd begun to believe in happily-ever-after. Once committed to that idea, a deepening of their physical involvement was a logical step in the progression toward... toward forever.

The more she thought about it, the more positive Hilary became that she had Matt pegged. He wanted their relationship neatly pigeonholed and labeled: marriage.

That was why she had to end things. She couldn't in good conscience encourage a doomed alliance, or encourage false hopes. Matt demanded that everything be in its place, and that probably included any wife he might acquire. "And I'm *never* in my place," she murmured aloud as she poured the boiling water over a tea bag. So even if she thought she'd be happy within the strict boundaries of a marriage, she didn't have the wherewithal to make Matt happy.

She couldn't bear the thought of him growing to resent her. She loved him too much for that. Perhaps it was because she loved him that she had to free him before they made a huge mistake. And this time, when she called it quits, she was determined to make it stick.

When she heard the front door open, she resisted the urge to hide. Instead she took a calming sip of her citrus tea, letting the warm liquid slide down her raw throat. She couldn't keep running away when things got too difficult. This was one problem she had to face, and the sooner the better.

Matt entered the kitchen, paused when he saw her, then continued on his path toward the refrigerator.

Hilary sat very still, waiting for him to make the first move.

"I won the log-splitting contest," he said cautiously.

She didn't doubt it. Matt had the best biceps on the block. She was sorry she'd missed seeing him in action, wielding an ax. Had he taken his shirt off to compete? Why did she have to think about that now? "Congratulations," she finally offered.

He poured himself a glass of ice water. "Are you coming back to join the party?"

"I don't think so."

Unruffled, he pulled out a chair and joined her at the kitchen table. "Then are you going to tell me what's wrong?"

His question was so gentle, so full of the will to understand, that Hilary wished she could melt into a little puddle and seep through the cracks in the linoleum. His anger she could deal with, but not this, not this compassion. She took a deep breath, praying she could keep the tears at bay this time. "A lot of things are wrong. I didn't mean to play games with you."

"That notion hadn't crossed my mind. Your distress was too genuine to be part of any game." He reached for her hand and placed it between both of his. "Why did you run away? Did I say something wrong? Do something wrong? Please, I can't help if I don't know what's upset you."

She couldn't think when he touched her, even in such an innocent fashion. Deliberately she pulled away from him, pushed her chair back and stood. She paced nervously about the small kitchen, wondering just how to put her thoughts into words, words that wouldn't sound harsh. "We aren't right for each other," she finally said.

"I see," he replied calmly. "What made you decide that?"

"We argue—"

"That won't wash anymore. We've always argued. We always manage to work things out, too. You can do better than that."

She shook her head. "You'll have to accept my decision in this. It couldn't have worked out."

Matt waited a long time before responding. Something had scared Hilary, and he still suspected that the possessive gleam in his eye had been the culprit. He thought back to what he'd almost said in the heat of his passion—something about making her his for all time?

That was a damn fool thing to say to a free spirit like Hilary. He'd have probably gotten the same result if he'd described the gilded cage he intended to put her in. She would always soar with a free-blowing wind; she would never belong to anyone.

Given her skittishness, the worst thing he could do was pressure her for answers, no matter how badly he wanted to understand her feelings. More subtle tactics were in order.

He went over his meager alternatives: He could argue with her, and try to make her understand how he felt and what permanence could mean to them both—and risk driving her further away. Or he could give her what she wanted, see if it made her happy—and hope she'd be miserable.

The choice wasn't difficult. When he had his strategy firmly in mind, Matt looked up at her, shrugged, and gave her a game smile. "All right, Hilary. Whatever you decide is fine. We don't have to go to bed. We don't even have to hold hands, if you don't want to. Why don't we just settle back and see what the rest of the summer brings?"

She couldn't have been more surprised if he'd sprouted a third eye in the middle of his forehead, though she quickly schooled her expression. She wanted to reply, but she didn't know quite what to make of this unexpected acquiescence.

"We'll just take things as they come," he added. "No pressure, no grand expectations."

She wanted to object, but what exactly could she object to when he was being so damned agreeable? So she waited cautiously.

"Are you sure you don't want to rejoin the block party? No, I guess you wouldn't," he said, answering his own question. "You look pretty drained."

"I am. But I'm also pretty hungry," she found herself saying. "I guess I could go long enough to eat some barbecue. Bob would be disappointed in me if I didn't have at least a couple of those ribs he's been bragging about."

Had she imagined the look of satisfaction that crossed Matt's face? But he turned away from her before she could be sure, to put his glass in the dishwasher. "Oh, before you go back to the party I want to show you something," he said, crooking his finger at her invitingly. "Come with me."

She couldn't have said no if she'd wanted to. She was numb from the range of emotions that had ravaged her psyche today, not the least of which was surprise over Matt's latest mood. She'd expected him to be angry over her decision to break things off between them. She'd expected an argument, or some sort of outburst. After all, wasn't that what a man did when the woman he wanted for his own told him to take a hike?

The last thing she'd ever expected Matthew Burke to do was agree with her. "Let's just take things as they come," he'd said. Such a happy-go-lucky sentiment went against everything he was—everything she thought he was, she amended. So much for her ability to second-guess Matt.

She followed him through the living room and out onto the patio, where he paused in front of his experimental roses. She'd grown accustomed to seeing them in their small pots, lined up on the patio or in the greenhouse. "Take a look at these," he said.

She bent down for a closer inspection. Buds! She couldn't help it; despite the way this abysmal day was turning out, a smile spread across her face. "So, your little hybrids are going to bloom."

Matt awarded her a silly grin. "Yup. Nearly every one has a bud now. Pretty soon I'll know if any of them show promise."

"And if they do? Do you have some sturdy root stock to graft them onto?" she asked, knowing at least that much about rose propagation. Hybrid tea roses seldom grew well on their own root systems.

"At home," Matt answered. "But I was going to ask you if you could spare a few cuttings from those guys." He inclined his head toward the garage, where the rosebushes grew healthy and free of aphids, but still bloomless. "I have a feeling your grandmother's roses would make fine root stock. I could get some canes started for next year."

"Sure, help yourself," Hilary answered, unwilling to look at the bare bushes. Somehow they reminded her of failure.

"They're just taking a summer hiatus," Matt said, reading her thoughts with uncanny accuracy. "They'll bloom again soon."

"I know." She tried to believe it, too.

They rejoined the party after that, and stayed until it began to wind down, close to midnight. They stuffed themselves with barbecue and the mulberry-lemon pie, which Sheila had thoughtfully removed from the oven before it burned. They talked trivialities and laughed at Bob's corny jokes. They even danced together to some Big Band music, though Hilary noticed that Matt made it a point not to hold her too close.

She tried not to regret her decision. She tried awfully damn hard.

"Feel free to sleep late tomorrow," Matt said a little later as they made their awkward good-nights at the top of the stairs. "There's not much going on in the garden." Usually he kissed her at this time. Tonight he didn't. Instead he gave her a jaunty salute and turned away from her, walking toward his room with a springy step.

Several minutes later, Hilary lay in bed and fumed silently. How dare he be so cheerful? But she was only mad at herself, she realized. *Sleep late tomorrow,* he'd said. If she hadn't botched things up so colossally, they could have slept late together.

Immediately she put a clamp on that line of thinking. Nothing had changed since this afternoon. She hadn't imagined those words he'd spoken to her...*real*... *solid*...*lasting*...*future*. He'd said all those things in the heat of desire. Could it be he hadn't meant them? He sure didn't act like a man whose hopes for the future had been dashed.

She should have felt tremendous relief that he was handling rejection so well. But all she could muster was vague disappointment and a sense of unease, as if everything she'd taken for granted was upside down and backward.

She punched her pillow and burrowed her head into it in an effort to get comfortable. But she might as well have been trying to sleep on a bed of nails. All she could think about was that Matt's door was just a few steps from her own. But though the temptation was strong, she couldn't give in. For as frivolous as she was about some things, sharing a bed with Matt couldn't be taken lightly. When they made love, she wanted them both to be very sure about what they were doing and what it meant.

What was wrong with her? Why was she suddenly the one who had to know where they were headed?

The next day Matt made the thirty-minute drive to Blue Springs so he could check on the progress of the remodeling and make some decisions regarding things like paint colors and bathroom tile.

A couple of months ago he'd been excited about the renovations. Now, as he viewed the mess being made of his house and greenhouse, he felt not even a twinge of anticipation about the finished product. He'd come to think of that funny pink house in Westport as his home. He could hardly envision himself moving back here.

Still, he applied himself to the various decisions he had to make. More than likely he *would* be moving back here, he reminded himself, and he'd just as soon not have to live with a pea-green living room—or worse.

He could have hurried his business and been done in a day, but since his bedroom was relatively livable, he decided to stretch his visit. Hilary would benefit from some time alone, he reasoned. In the back of his mind, however, was a notion not quite so noble. He was hoping she might miss him, and perhaps come to realize that she enjoyed having him around even if they didn't always get along. He missed *her*, more than he liked to admit.

When he finally returned to Westport, he was as anxious as if he'd been gone for weeks, though he had no idea what reception to expect from Hilary. What he got was like nothing he would have guessed. As soon as he pulled his car in the driveway, she burst out the front door and raced toward him, her face animated with excitement.

"Oh, I'm so glad you're finally home," she said breathlessly, all but pulling him out of the car. "I tried to call you earlier at the number you left, but I kept getting a phone company recording."

"The contractor accidentally cut through a line yesterday," Matt explained, following her at a fast clip around the side of the house. "Is something wrong?"

"Wrong? No. I didn't mean to alarm you. It's the roses."

"Which ones?" he asked.

"The babies. The buds are opening. I was afraid you'd miss it."

He'd seen thousands of rosebuds open, probably hundreds that were the result of his cross-pollinization experiments. But when Hilary dragged him onto the patio, then practically pushed his face into the burgeoning blooms, he really saw them for the first time, through her fresh eyes. New life. A new start.

"I see them," he said with a chuckle.

"Aren't they wonderful?"

"Yes," he agreed. "They're doing just what they're supposed to do. In another few days we can evaluate the results." His gaze strayed from the roses to her flushed, anxious face and back again. He hated not being able to touch her. Did she have any idea how soft and desirable she looked right now? The roses paled in comparison.

He forced his attention back to the flowers, to one bloom in particular. It was an eye-popping scarlet with streaks of pink. The flower was large, perfectly formed, thick with petals. The plant itself appeared sturdy, with dark green, waxy leaves.

"I noticed that one, too," said Hilary, following his gaze. "Is it special?"

"Could be. I think it bears watching."

Hilary did watch it, every chance she got. Whenever she walked outside, her eyes immediately searched for the rose pots. Sometimes they were on the patio, sometimes in the greenhouse under the grow lights. When she found them, she would visit the tiny roses and talk to them, urging them to grow and be beautiful. She always spared an extra word of encouragement for the one promising rose.

She wasn't sure why the struggling plants were suddenly so important to her. If the lack of blooms on Grandma's roses symbolized failure, perhaps these little flowers, so fresh and optimistic, meant a new beginning—another chance for herself and Matt. Maybe it wasn't too late for her to change her mind about a few things.

During the two days Matt had been gone, she'd alternately cursed the man for coming into her life in the first place, and prayed that he would come back soon because his absence was downright painful. When he *had* come back, and his return had coincided so perfectly with the blooming, she'd felt encouraged, as if providence was on her side. Maybe she was being silly, but she believed in her heart that this business with the roses had some deep significance.

Though their physical involvement had come to a screeching halt, their relationship was changing in other, more positive ways. The mutual criticism had stopped, and so had the arguments. In their place was a new degree of tolerance. Matt allowed a dish or two to sit in the sink for longer than ten minutes. He let laundry pile up. Once, he used the hose and didn't coil it up afterward. Hilary, trying to get in the spirit of things, had coiled it up for him when he wasn't looking. Then she'd done a load of laundry and had tried to fold the towels exactly the way Matt liked them.

They had talked, really talked, more than they had all summer. Hilary learned about Matt's family. His father was an engineer and his mother had won national awards for her counted cross-stitch. He had an older brother who was a dentist. "Now you know where I got it from," he'd said after describing his family, "it" referring to his penchant for neatness and precision.

Hilary told him about her mother, who had died so young, and the mysterious father she never knew. She told him about the rare, close relationship that had developed between herself and her grandmother as they shared their grief. She even told him about her disastrous engagement to Stephen, and he shared with her an equally dismal love affair he'd had in college.

And so things went for a few days, slowly, cautiously, but with growing optimism—until one sultry morning when Hilary wandered onto the patio to drink her morning coffee. It was hot, humid and still, and a menacing bank of steely gray clouds were gathering in the southwest. She'd heard on the radio that a storm was on the way, and had gone outside to check the conditions and see about taking precautions to protect the garden. Then she saw the rose—one lonely little rose plant in a large pot without its compatriots.

"Where did your friends go?" she asked the wilting scarlet and pink bloom. Thinking that perhaps they were in the greenhouse, Hilary went to investigate, taking the lone rose with her as if to reunite it with its brothers and sisters. But she found no neat rows of pots in there, either. Deciding the greenhouse was the best place to leave the rose during a storm, she set the plastic pot on a bench and turned to leave, intent on finding Matt and asking him where the other roses were. Then she saw a flash of pink from the corner of her eye.

The color was peeking out of the top of the garbage can. Curious, Hilary stepped closer to the can as a sense of dread enveloped her. *It can't be,* she thought as she pulled the lid off the garbage can.

An involuntary cry escaped from her throat at the sight that greeted her—a tangle of wilted greenery, bare roots, and red and pink blooms, with potting soil clinging to everything.

"How could he do this?" she asked aloud as she reached for one of the discarded flowers. She shook the potting soil off, then brought it close to her face so she could smell the faint scent.

She could repot them, she thought through a mist of sentimentality. But they probably wouldn't live. Still, she couldn't let them die without a little dignity. So she located a pair of pruning shears and methodically began picking through the trash, clipping the blooms from the wilting plants and laying them gently on a bench. Salvaging all but the ones that were downright dead, she filled a jar with water and stuck the flowers into it. The arrangement was bedraggled at best, she conceded with a sniff. She was still glad she'd done it. She wrapped the rest of the greenery in newspaper and laid it gently in the trash.

Matt picked that moment to stride into the greenhouse, whistling cheerfully, obviously full of purpose.

"You!" The single word brought him up short. Hilary was standing about ten feet in front of him, pointing the garden shears at him menacingly.

"Me?" He pointed to his chest.

"You, you Nazi!" She slammed the metal lid of the garbage can down with a deafening crash. "How could you do it? How could you kill them?"

"Kill who?" But then he saw the jar with its droopy bouquet, and he understood—all too well. He'd really done it this time. "Oh," was all he could manage to say.

"Yeah, 'Oh.' How could you just throw the baby roses into the garbage as if they mean nothing?"

"But they've served their purpose," he argued reasonably. "They were weak specimens. They weren't meant to grow up."

"So you toss them away just because they aren't pretty enough for you? I suppose you believe in drowning mongrel puppies, too."

"I do not. That's entirely different."

"How do you know it's different?" she demanded. "No one's proved plants can feel, but no one's proved they can't, either."

He sighed hopelessly. "I can't argue with that. But what did you expect me to do, give them a funeral? I can't keep them all, or I'd be running a rose orphanage."

"I'm not suggesting you keep them indefinitely. But every living thing ought to serve some purpose before it dies," she said, pointing to the limp bouquet. "You didn't have to throw out the flowers so carelessly. They were still pretty. We could have enjoyed them a few days longer."

"You're right," he agreed, feeling more and more like the heartless heel she painted him to be. He should have thought about Hilary's feelings, if not those of the roses. Though he might never view plants in the personal way she did, he could have waited a little longer before discarding the weak roses. And he could have done it with more sensitivity.

Despite his capitulation, Hilary's tirade continued. He gazed at her, not really hearing her words anymore but feeling a tide of emotion pouring from her. God, she was sincere. She was hurting, and he was responsible.

He knew then that he loved her. How could he not love a woman who felt compassion for the lowliest roses, and who could also make him regret mistreating them? She made him feel things he never imagined. She gave life a whole new definition.

"Don't just stand there gaping at me, dammit," she said at last when he'd failed to respond. "I want you to explain to me how you can nurture something for more than two months, water it, feed it, agonize over it, rejoice when it blooms, then toss it aside when it's not useful or convenient anymore."

Suddenly Matt had the eerie feeling they were talking about more than just roses. Maybe it was time for him to push a little. "I might ask you the same question," he said slowly, fixing her with a meaningful stare. "For weeks we struggled to work things out between us, and just when it was all coming together, you were willing to toss what we had aside. Why?" He drew one step closer to her.

A wary look came into her eyes. She stiffened and crossed her arms in a protective gesture. "Why are you bringing that up now?"

Before he could reply, thunder clapped violently outside, rattling the panes of the greenhouse. A gust of wind suddenly whipped through the open door, cooling flushed skin, cooling tempers.

Hilary swallowed visibly. The wariness in her eyes receded, leaving nothing except naked vulnerability. "I was afraid," she finally answered.

"Afraid of what?" he asked gently, moving close enough to touch her, though he didn't.

"That you wanted to marry me," she blurted out. "Everything you said in the span of a minute or two smacked of permanence. I wasn't ready for it."

"Ah." He nodded understanding. He'd guessed correctly, then. "A fate worse than death, being married to me?"

"I told you once, I'm lousy wife material." She stared down at her pink-polished toenails, then back up at him with big, soft gray-green eyes.

He knew when to pull back. "You don't have to look at me like a rabbit in a snare. I have no intention of tying you down."

"If not marriage, then what did you...what *do* you have in mind?" she asked, so softly he barely understood her words.

She'd mistaken the meaning of what he said, but for now he would let her cling to her illusions. He took a deep breath, knowing he wouldn't tell her the whole truth. "Just to make love, Hilary. We've shared a lot this summer. I feel closer to you than I have to any woman. I want to feel even closer."

His words gentled her. The apprehension left her eyes, and her posture relaxed. She reached out a hand for him, and he took it. "I'm so tired of talking, Matt. So tired of trying to figure things out."

"Amen to that. Even *my* scientist's brain has had enough critical analysis." He drew her willingly into the circle of his arms and laid his cheek against her coppery hair. For a long time they stood like that, holding each other silently, breathing in unison. The greenhouse smelled of fertile soil and traces of the lush, burgeoning life that had so recently occupied it.

When another gust of wind blew through the greenhouse, it brought more than rain with it. The damp air caressing Matt's skin touched off a flood of desire.

Suddenly nothing mattered but Hilary. He wanted her. He needed her. He desperately needed the closeness making love to her would bring. If he didn't dare tell her in words the depth of his feelings, he could show her. Never had it been so important to reaffirm everything that was good and right between them.

When he moved to claim a kiss, her face was already upturned, ready to receive him. Their lips met with a silent explosion that rivaled the thunder. He clutched at her thick, soft hair, twining it around his fingers with one hand while the other sought the unforgettable feel of her breast.

She moaned when he touched her. God, she was magnificent, all fire and trembling warmth. He yearned to see the treasures she hid beneath her clothes. As if reading his thoughts, she pulled away from him and peeled her T-shirt over her head in one graceful, brazen movement. She allowed him one tantalizing glimpse of her firm breasts encased in a scrap of silk and lace before moving into his embrace again.

He ached to possess her. He'd never wanted anything so badly.

She started to tug impatiently at his T-shirt, and he reluctantly let her go so she could bare his chest. As soon as he was free of the garment, he held her close again, reveling in the feel of skin against skin. He leaned down to plant a chain of kisses along her collarbone, then let his tongue dip into and tease the cleft between her breasts.

She let out a tiny gasp. "Matt, we can't make love here."

"Why not?" he growled, paying homage to the hollow at the base of her throat.

"The walls are glass. The neighbors are nosy. And there's not anything remotely soft—oh, do that again—to lie down on."

He chuckled softly as he shifted his attention to her ear. "We could do it standing up."

"Matt!"

He wasn't sure if she was commenting on his suggestion or the fact that he was teasing her ear with his tongue. At any rate, a patter of small hail overhead reminded him that their choice of a love nest was less than perfect.

He'd take care of that, and quickly before either of them came to their senses. He scooped Hilary into his arms and carried her out of the greenhouse door, heedless of her laughing protest. But as soon as they were outside, they were pelted by a cold, hard rain and pea-sized hail. Favoring speed over chivalry, he let her down and they both dashed under the shelter of the patio overhang.

Moisture clung to Hilary's hair and her eyelashes, and made her skin into shiny gold satin. The hardened buds of her nipples pushed at the sheer fabric that contained them, renewing Matt's desire instantaneously.

She shivered, from desire and from the chilled wind whipping against her wet skin. "Let's get inside," she said, fearful of speaking and shattering the mood. But Matt's intentions were sure and unwavering, as were hers. With their arms around each other, they made slow progress up the stairs and into her bedroom, stopping to kiss and caress every few steps.

As soon as the door was closed, Hilary eagerly shimmied out of her shorts, glorying in the way Matt's eyes lit up with approval. He reached for her again, as if he couldn't bear any space at all separating them, but before he could pull her too close, she grasped the waistband of his cutoffs and saucily flipped open the top button.

"I've dreamed about taking these ridiculously skimpy things off you since the moment I first saw you wear them," she declared, flicking the second button open. The feel of his arousal pushing against his briefs made her even more bold.

She was working on the third button, to the accompaniment of Matt's uneven breathing, when something like an explosion and the sound of shattering glass froze her movements. For a moment they were suspended in time, still as porcelain figurines, until Matt breathed the words.

"The greenhouse."

Chapter Nine

Hilary yanked open her dresser drawer and threw on the first T-shirt she could find, but by the time she was dressed, Matt was already downstairs. She found him on the patio, staring glassy-eyed at a scene of unrelenting destruction. A bolt of lightning had neatly cleaved the neighbor's century-old oak tree, half of which had fallen through the fence and onto the greenhouse. The fragile house of glass had smashed as if it were made of nothing but sugar cubes. A peculiar electrical smell still hung in the air.

Hilary wasn't sure which was worse—the devastation to her backyard, or the hard expression on Matt's face as he stood, grave and unyielding as a granite wall, while the angry wind and rain whipped against his bare torso.

She said the first comforting words that came to mind. "It could have been a lot worse. At least the greenhouse wasn't full of plants. And I have lots of insurance, so anything you did lose can be replaced..." If Matt heard her stream of chatter, he made no indication. So she fell silent and stood beside him to watch the storm release the last of its rage.

When the rain had dwindled to a sprinkle twenty minutes later and the skies had lightened, Hilary took a visual inventory of the damage. The yard was a surrealistic fantasyland littered with jagged shards of glass and smooth, round hailstones, some of them almost as big as golf balls. The odd images of clear and shiny, white and dull, mixed with bits of green grass and festooned with water droplets was almost beautiful.

But the fantasy took on nightmarish aspects as Hilary allowed reality to sink in. At least half the greenhouse was a loss, not to mention the fine old oak tree. The test garden was badly damaged. Dozens of green tomatoes lay on the ground beneath battered and broken plants. Even the rosebushes looked beaten, though she knew they'd survive as they had countless other storms.

A chilling thought entered her mind: if she and Matt hadn't left the greenhouse when they did...but they had, she reminded herself. No sense in dwelling on morbid possibilities. She should be thanking the heavens that nothing much at all was in the greenhouse—except the baby rose.

Suddenly she had to know how the lone survivor had fared. "I'm going to check the damage," she said, starting toward the greenhouse.

"Hilary!" The sharp utterance halted her. "Put some shoes on, for Pete's sake. There's glass everywhere."

She looked down at her feet, surprised to see they were bare. At least Matt had broken out of his trancelike silence, she thought, though she'd rather he didn't bark at her. What had happened to the tenderness he'd shown her only minutes ago? He acted as if this disaster were somehow her fault.

She gave him a reproachful look as she passed, but he was no longer paying any attention to her. He was again staring stonily at the ravaged yard.

When Matt heard the patio door close behind him, he let out a deep breath. *God Almighty, look at this place.* What had he been thinking?

He hadn't been thinking at all. He'd been so focused on Hilary that he'd ceased to be rational. His mind had been full to the brim with thoughts of making love with her; those thoughts had left little room for other concerns, such as protecting his garden and his rose from the storm.

He'd lost control.

He'd never learned to tolerate anyone's loss of control, but especially not his own. Even now he lacked his usual decision-making abilities. He was floundering, and he had no idea how to deal with it.

He forced himself to look on the devastation, almost as a self-punishment for his lack of foresight. His garden was a wasteland. He walked about in the yard, his hands shoved into the pockets of his cutoffs. He angrily kicked a green tomato, but the gesture only made him feel empty and powerless.

The final blow came when he entered the greenhouse to view the havoc. One of the first things he saw was the green plastic pot that was home to his one promising rose. It had spilled onto the concrete floor, dumping its contents. The plant was broken off at the roots.

He scooped up the mangled plant with the pot, then dropped the whole mess into the garbage can. When he looked up again, he realized Hilary was there, watching in sympathetic silence.

He didn't want her sympathy, dammit. Right now he wanted no part of her. It wasn't that he blamed her for this disaster. But it was Hilary who had distracted him. It was she who'd turned his brain into mush. If he let her near him, if he accepted the comfort she offered, he'd lose himself again, and he didn't want that right now.

"Can't the rose be salvaged?" she asked in a tiny voice.

"No. It's dead."

She flinched at the finality of his words. He hated himself for causing her pain, but he knew that one soft word from him would send her flying into his arms. He wouldn't be able to deny her, or himself, that closeness.

Apparently he'd succeeded in keeping her at bay. She withdrew quietly from the greenhouse and left him to his self-damning thoughts.

When he walked back outside a few minutes later, the sun was peeking through thinning clouds. Birds were bathing in the puddles and calling to one another with a cheerfulness that seemed to mock the grim scene.

Hilary was gathering up the green tomatoes into a basket. "I can make green-tomato chutney," she said by way of explanation when Matt gave her a curious look. Naturally, she'd come up with a use for the immature tomatoes, he thought with a surge of affection. She wouldn't want the plants to have lived and died without serving some purpose, or the fruit to go to waste.

But his research project *was* a waste, he acknowledged. He'd send the seed company an abbreviated report and ask them to pay him whatever they thought it was worth. It didn't matter. What did matter was that with the end of the tomato plants came the end of his need to stay in Hilary's house.

They spent the next several hours cleaning up the mess in the steamy afternoon heat. To Hilary, the time dragged as if it were days. She'd tried to coax Matt out of his brooding silence, but he seemed determined to remain mad at the world. Finally she gave up trying, and without the distraction of conversation, the cleanup tasks became all the more tedious.

She tried to tell herself that Matt was only upset over the loss of his garden and his rose. But deep down she knew there was more to his mood. He was deliberately distancing himself from her, and she had no idea what she'd done to deserve his coolness. Disasters were supposed to draw people closer together, weren't they?

Eventually Matt would reveal what troubled him, she guessed. But still she wore herself down trying to figure out what misdeed of hers had put him in this dark frame of mind, and how to bring him out of it.

Midafternoon Bob and another neighbor brought over chainsaws to reduce the fallen tree to firewood. While the three men worked on that chore, Hilary collected broken glass and smaller branches into boxes and bags and set them out by the curb. By evening the yard looked almost presentable. But Hilary's heart felt like a lead weight inside her chest. Matt could talk and laugh with the men who helped with the tree, but he couldn't spare even a small smile for her.

When there was no work left to do, she threw together some sandwiches while Matt took a shower. He thanked her tersely when she handed him a plate, then picked at the food as his mind obviously wandered elsewhere. Though Hilary had eaten nothing all day, she could choke down no more than a couple of bites.

"I have to go," Matt announced abruptly, pushing his plate aside.

"Go where?" she asked, but even before the question was out she'd guessed the answer.

"Away from here. I need to think."

"Why can't you think here? I won't bother you." She knew she argued in vain, but she couldn't help herself. The thought of living here in this house alone was intolerable.

"You will bother me," he said, though when her eyes widened in surprise at his harsh words he shook his head and apologized. "I didn't mean that the way it sounded. I don't want you to think I'm angry with you. I'm more angry with myself, for wanting you so badly."

She shook her head in confusion.

He tried again. "You're so sweet and sexy and desirable, Hilary, and when you're around I want you all the time. That's the problem. I haven't had a clear head in weeks. I need to think some place where you aren't around to distract me."

"Why is it a problem that you want me?" she asked, latching on to the one thing he'd said that most baffled her.

"Because...because I want you to the exclusion of everything else. I've completely lost my perspective, my logic, my common sense. My life doesn't seem to be my own anymore. Somewhere along the line I lost control of who I am and where I'm going."

"And the storm made you realize that?" she asked, struggling to comprehend.

"Don't you see? Much of the storm damage could have been prevented if I'd devoted a single brain cell to something other than...other than you."

"Matt, not even you could have prevented lightning from striking that tree."

"No, but I could have sheltered the garden from the hail. I could have brought the little rose into the house. Normally I would have done both of those things as a matter of course when I heard the severe storm was headed our way. But instead . . ."

"Instead you made a mistake. A small error in judgment. So what? You aren't perfect, though I imagine you'd like to be." She picked up their plates and emptied the leftovers into the trash.

"I don't expect perfection of myself. But neither do I enjoy making careless, costly mistakes just because I'm . . . I'm distracted."

One of the plates slipped from her grasp and crashed to the floor. "Well, thanks a heap. I'm glad it meant so much to you."

"Oh, God, Hilary, I didn't mean—"

"Go ahead and leave," she said, cutting off his apology. "But don't plan on coming back."

He challenged her with a stare that should by all rights have reduced her to tears. But she returned his gaze steadily, daring him to argue with her further. At least arguing was preferable to that deathly silence he'd treated her to most of the day. In the end it was he who looked away first, muttering a curse under his breath as he left the table.

He had his car packed to the roof in a matter of minutes. But by the time he was ready to leave, Hilary's temper had cooled enough that she managed to walk outside to where he was stuffing one last armload of clothes into the trunk in a most un-Matt-like fashion. She was still furious at what he'd said, but she could see that Matt was hurting, too.

"I left a few things behind," he said as he tied down the lid to his overflowing trunk with a piece of cord. "I'll send someone for them."

This wasn't what she wanted. She swallowed a lump of pride in her throat before speaking. "Matt, I know you didn't mean to sound callous. I didn't mean what I said, either. If you want to, after you've had time to think, you can always come back here."

He almost smiled at her then, the first time he'd come even close since the storm. "I'll keep that in mind. It's more than I deserve."

She held on to the hope that he really did intend to sort out his feelings, that he wasn't planning to simply leave her and wipe the summer's events from his mind. She summoned a *c'est la vie* smile for him when he handed her his set of keys to her house, even though she wanted more than anything to cry. She managed to hold her tears in check just until his car pulled around the corner and out of sight.

Hilary went about her business for the next few days, trying not to believe that her whole world had shifted off its axis and was spinning wildly off course. She met with her insurance adjuster and haggled with him over her claim. She attended a school faculty meeting and put in her preferences for her next year's teaching responsibilities. She made green-tomato chutney. She dabbled with her paints, purposely avoiding the picture of Matt.

The only thing that really held her interest was gardening. Despite the beating it had received, the garden was actually doing quite well. Several of the tomato plants had survived, some of them with fruit intact, and she tended them with all the loving care she could muster. She even took some halfhearted notes on their growth, though she knew she'd have no earthly use for them. She just didn't like seeing the tomato project abandoned before it was finished, she supposed.

When the immediate pain of Matt's sudden departure eased a little, she tried to look back objectively at their time together and figure out what she could have done differently. She could have learned to properly coil a garden hose, she mused one hot afternoon as she absently pulled her school art supplies out of the upstairs hall closet. She could have tried harder to control her runaway temper. She could have put up with largest-to-smallest, left-to-right, and not complained so much.

But upon reflection, she realized that Matt's reason for leaving her had little to do with her behavior and everything to do with her influence over *his* behavior. She'd caused him to act irresponsibly, to lose the rigid control he'd previously held over himself and his surroundings. That loss of control had so disturbed him that he'd fled from it.

There wasn't a thing she could do to help him work it out, she thought glumly. He'd have to come to grips with the problem all on his own. She was haunted by the fear that he might simply refuse to deal with it, to turn his back on everything that had happened and return to the comfortable life he'd had before.

Struggling to dismiss Matt from her mind for at least the hundredth time that day, she laid out her supply of art materials on the hall floor, taking inventory of what she had left from last year and jotting down what she would need to buy. Surely she had more construction paper than this, she thought. She'd bought a big carton of the stuff only last year—ah, now she remembered. She'd stored it in the attic.

The door to the attic was directly above her. She pulled the cord that dangled from the trapdoor in the ceiling, then lowered the folding staircase that gave her access to the small, stuffy space. Waves of hot air washed over her as she ascended the stairs. She stepped onto the rough, wooden flooring and flipped on the light, half-expecting to see stacks and rows of identical cartons. She almost would have welcomed the sight, she realized with a twinge of surprise. But this was obviously one area Matt hadn't touched. It was a wreck.

Fifty years' worth of treasures and trash alike lay in heaps that climbed as high as the rafters. Hilary wrinkled her nose at the musty smell as she wondered where she might have stashed the construction paper. Her eyes traveled over battered boxes, piles of discarded clothing, old toys and ugly lamps before coming to rest on a decrepit bookcase. There she spotted not the paper carton she sought, but the elusive red binders—her grandmother's gardening notebooks.

With a prickling of excitement, Hilary picked her way across the cluttered attic to the bookcase, where the notebooks lay stacked on a shelf just as she'd once pictured them in her mind. And to think she'd almost emptied every box in the basement searching for something that wasn't there.

She pulled the whole stack down into her arms, then found a comfortable, albeit dusty, seat in a tattered pink easy chair. The binders were dated, so it was simple to find the most recent one. With growing anticipation, she leafed through it until she came to the section labeled "Spring Sunrise."

Her grandmother had recorded the flower's lineage, the date and procedure she'd used in cross-pollinating the parent blooms, and drawings of several flowers produced by the match—all of them apparently discarded except for the spectacular yellow blossom with the orange center.

The scope and detail of the recorded data astounded Hilary. The pages could almost have come from Matt's notebook, they were so meticulously done, indicating a penchant for neatness and organization Hilary never would have guessed. Had she inherited any of these qualities from her grandmother? she wondered. Were they there but hidden so deeply she hadn't found them yet?

Quickly she thumbed to the final pages of the binder, where her grandmother had noted the distribution of her roses in preparation for the death she'd known was imminent. Hilary found the answer she sought almost immediately and was stunned by the words she read in the shaky, spidery script. The Spring Sunrise had been right under her nose the whole time.

School art supplies were forgotten as she rushed down two flights of stairs and out the front door. She didn't break stride until she arrived at the screen door to Sheila's kitchen. Taking a calming breath, she rapped sharply and called out a greeting.

"Come on in," Sheila answered over her shoulder. She was standing at the sink, elbow-deep in sudsy water. "Your timing is faultless. You just missed helping me feed watermelon to a kitchen full of orangutans... Bryan's neighborhood friends, that is."

"I wish you'd called me," said Hilary, automatically picking up a dish towel and drying the plates stacked in the drainer. She'd get around to asking about the rose, but first she'd be neighborly. She'd avoided Sheila the last few days, reluctant to answer questions about Matt the other woman would undoubtedly ask.

"I wasn't sure you were up to visiting," Sheila said cautiously. "Or am I just imagining that I haven't seen Matt's car in over a week?"

"You weren't imagining. And I was feeling antisocial for a while, but at this point my own company has become rather tedious."

"Oh, honey, I'm sorry—"

Hilary held up her hand to halt Sheila. "Please, don't." She forced a smile. "Honestly, I'm going to survive this." Brave words, she thought, for someone who was barely coping with a vast hollowness in her life.

Sheila gave her a sideways glance of sympathy. "The rat," she muttered. "I'm going to tell his mother."

"It's not really his fault," Hilary said. "Blame it on a personality conflict. It couldn't have worked in the long run."

"Try a little harder and you might convince me of that. But you'll never convince yourself."

"No, really," Hilary insisted. "We're just too different. Matt's so, you know, and I'm so..."

"In love with him?" Sheila suggested.

Hilary sighed hopelessly. "Yeah. Guess you're right."

Sheila put her arm around Hilary and gave her shoulder a wet, soapy squeeze. "Don't lose faith. Maybe after he stews in his own juices for a while he'll come to his senses."

He's already come to his senses, Hilary thought as she dried the last plate. That was the problem. Matthew Burke was altogether too sensible for his own good.

"So did you drop by for any particular reason?" Sheila asked, wiping her hands on her apron.

Hilary was grateful for the change of subject. "Yes, as a matter of fact. Did Grandma give you her Spring Sunrise rosebush before she died?"

Sheila's face brightened. "Yes, she did. I'd forgotten that she called it 'Spring Sunrise.' What about it?"

"Grandma developed it herself. Matt saw a picture of it, and he thinks it might be valuable. He wants to work with it, maybe take it to a commercial rose grower. I'd like to buy it back from you, Sheila."

Sheila's hands went to her hips. "What, and give it to Matt the rat?"

"It's the least I could do. I feel partly responsible for the destruction of a promising rose he was growing. I'm the one who put it in the greenhouse where it got smashed."

Sheila relented. "The rose is all yours if it's important to you. I've never had much luck with roses. But there is a slight problem..." She hung her apron on the refrigerator door. "C'mon, let's go see." She led Hilary into the backyard, where an untidy grouping of ten or twelve rosebushes huddled against the privacy fence. None of them were blooming.

"I didn't realize you grew roses," Hilary said, examining the plants.

Sheila laughed. "I don't. I planted your grandmother's rose, and then Bob decided it looked silly all by itself, so he went to the nursery and bought a bunch more to plant with it. Then some of them died... Anyway, Bob keeps bringing them home from the nursery, and I keep killing them off with my brown thumb. I'm lucky if I manage to get even a few scraggly blooms."

"You mean, you don't know which one it is?" Hilary asked.

"That's the problem. I don't remember exactly where I planted it. It's one of those in the center... I think, unless... oh, I hope it wasn't one of the ones that died. You don't recognize it, either?"

Hilary shook her head, disappointed beyond words.

"We'll just have to wait till they bloom again," Sheila said cheerfully.

"Lord knows when that might be," Hilary mumbled, having become all too familiar with the vagaries of rose blooms. "I'll give you some of Matt's special rose food," she added. "Maybe that will kick the bushes into gear."

For a week Matt had wandered around in a fog of his own confusion, but finally the murkiness in his brain was beginning to lift and awareness was setting in. He looked around the main room of the tiny cabin he'd rented at Tomahawk Lake and suddenly realized he was living in a pigsty.

He had tried moving back to his own home. But the noise and dust from the contractors' work had driven him out within a day. Then he'd thought about moving in with his parents for a week or two, but he hadn't been in the mood for their questions or the regimented decor of their colonial home. The perfectly proportioned rooms, all in designer shades of beige, would only have made him miss Hilary's crazy-quilt decor all the more.

So a lake cabin had seemed the answer—total solitude, no phones or TV, just tons of time to get his head screwed on straight. But he hadn't done much thinking, he reflected. Mostly he'd just stared out at the water, feeling sorry for himself.

He rubbed his beard-stubbled jaw, idly wondering if he'd even brought a razor with him. He started to pick up the clothes thrown willy-nilly about the room. But he soon tired of the effort and collapsed into a flattened yellow beanbag chair to brood some more.

He hadn't seen Hilary in eight days, yet her presence was so vivid in his memory it was almost as if she were there with him. Visions of her gave him no comfort, however. If anything, the pain of leaving her had only intensified.

He'd been an idiot to believe that removing himself from the situation would put things back to the way they were three months ago. His time with Hilary had put an indelible mark on him. He was permanently changed, for better or worse, and there was no going back. The woman had altered his priorities until he wasn't certain what was important anymore. All he knew for sure was that he hurt, deep down, and the pain wasn't easing up.

Only one thing would cure that pain, and she was just a phone call away. He had a strong urge to run down the street to the pay phone at the QuikTrip. But the last thing he wanted to do was fly off half-cocked, saying and doing impulsive things. He'd done enough of that already. He couldn't risk hurting Hilary again. This time he had to be very sure—

Ah, hell, he'd *never* be that sure. Strong emotion wasn't something that could be measured, cataloged, and predicted. If he and Hilary ever got back together, unpredictability would reign. He'd find it in her, in himself, and in the path their life together would take. Sometimes they'd still drive each other crazy and have silly arguments. Sometimes Matt would doubt his own sanity as well as hers. They wouldn't even be married, unless Hilary changed her mind.

Could he handle all that uncertainty? Could he handle the fact that some questions about himself might go unanswered? Could he survive living with her?

He rolled his hand into a fist and punched a dent into the beanbag. Maybe he should be asking himself, could he live without her?

Chapter Ten

Hilary awoke early one morning feeling strangely optimistic. For the first time in the two weeks since Matt's abrupt departure, she looked forward to the prospect of getting out of bed. The thought of Matt still produced a sharp stab of pain in her heart, but it was accompanied by an inexplicable sense of anticipation.

Unwilling to examine too closely the reasons for her change of mood, in case she should break the spell and feel miserable again, she pushed herself out of bed, dressed quickly in gym shorts and a tank top, then went downstairs to get a jump on the garden before the sun got too high.

The first thing she was forced to do was untangle the hose. "Darn it, Matt, you were right all along," she muttered as she unbent one kink, only to have another one form. "A man would have to be crazy to stay with a woman who did this to him every day."

As she turned on the faucet and aimed a spray of water toward the surviving tomato plants, two workmen arrived to reconstruct the greenhouse.

"It'll only take a few days to build it better than new," one of them assured her. If only relationships were so easy to rebuild, she thought wistfully.

When the tomatoes were adequately soaked, she redirected the spray toward the rosebushes, which hadn't had a good drink in days. She could have simply laid the hose on the ground at the base of the bushes and let the water run unattended, she supposed, but she liked the feeling she got from actively watering her plants. It gave her time to look them over and give them a little verbal encouragement. Besides, when school started in another couple of weeks she wouldn't have the luxury of time for dawdling like this.

"So how are you this morning, my bloomless wonders?" she asked the roses. "Would you like some of Matt's special rose foo—" The last word stuck in her throat as her nerveless fingers dropped the hose. It flipped over and gave her a good dousing, but she hardly noticed.

Buds. Dozens and dozens of them, covering the bushes from top to bottom. They clustered on every branch, round and fat and ready to burst.

Hilary touched first one bud and then another, as if to reassure herself that she wasn't hallucinating. She pressed her face into the waxy leaves and inhaled deeply, anticipating the sweet, heavy scent that would come when the buds opened. Oh, this was marvelous!

They would need lots of water. She picked up the forgotten hose and let the flow soak the roots of the bushes. "You can have all the water you want, guys," she said, her voice squeaky with excitement. "I'll feed you, too.

I'll even play some Mozart. You deserve anything you want."

She gave in to the urge to laugh out loud—she couldn't remember ever feeling this giddy. The profusion of buds could mean only one thing: Matt was coming back to her. She was sure of it, more sure than she'd been about anything in her life.

She finished up the yard work with a soaring heart. Even the odious task of weeding seemed pleasurable in her euphoric state, and mowing the grass was a snap.

When all of the garden tools were put back just so and the hose meticulously coiled, Hilary went inside with a light step to see about breakfast. She had waffles in mind—or something equally fattening and full of carbohydrates. Given her current energy level, she'd burn it off in no time. But as soon as she saw the state of her kitchen, she forgot all about eating. How had she let it get so messy? A herd of elephants could have stampeded through and it wouldn't have looked much worse. She launched herself into a frenzy of cleaning.

In the past two weeks she'd hardly given a thought to housework, so she knew the rest of the house was as chaotic as the kitchen. Matt would get one look at this place and turn tail, she thought, scrubbing at a spot in the sink with renewed vigor. She scoured and polished and dusted for hours on end. She straightened and organized everything from the refrigerator to the fireplace mantle to the medicine cabinet. She trimmed all the dead leaves off her houseplants and lined up the pots from tallest to shortest, left to right. She washed and folded every sheet and towel in the house, then made her bed with hospital corners.

When she'd performed every conceivable chore, she looked at her watch and frowned. Almost seven o'clock.

Aside from the fact that she was starved, she was also a little disappointed. Matt hadn't arrived yet.

"But he will," she said aloud to bolster herself.

Sheila called to ask Hilary if she wanted to take in a late movie.

"I can't, I have to get ready," Hilary answered breathlessly. "Matt's coming home."

"Oh, that's terrific news," Sheila responded with a squeal of obvious delight. "So he finally came to his senses. When did he call?"

"Well, he didn't exactly call..."

"What'd he do, send you a postcard?"

"Grandma's roses are blooming," Hilary said, as if that explained everything.

"Huh?"

"I'll tell you all about it someday, Sheila. But he is coming back, I know he is. And I have to get ready—I'm a mess."

"If you say so, dear," Sheila said soothingly, as if talking to someone in the advanced stages of dementia. "You let me know how it all turns out."

After Hilary hung up, she wolfed down two pieces of cold pizza so that she wouldn't keel over from starvation. Then she applied the same concerted effort toward herself as she had the house. She scrubbed her lightly tanned skin until it glowed. She shampooed, dried and styled her hair with unusual care. She donned her sexiest lingerie, an ivory silk teddy with matching peignoir. She polished her fingernails in soft pink lacquer, then did her toenails for good measure. She applied her most expensive scent to every pulse point she knew of and a few she'd made up. The man wouldn't stand a chance of escaping her a second time.

All of these preparations occupied her until almost ten o'clock. A ghoulish horror paperback held her attention for a while longer. But at midnight, she was forced to acknowledge that she'd been wrong. Matt wasn't coming back after all.

With a heart as heavy as lead, she set a fan in the window and climbed into bed. As she turned off her bedside lamp, she tried to tell herself that Matt would arrive tomorrow, or the next day. After all, the rosebushes wouldn't be in full bloom for a while yet. There was plenty of time. But just the same, a silent tear trickled from the corner of her eye and dampened the pillow beneath her cheek.

Sometime later she was awakened by a noise. She shot upright and held her breath to listen, but the only sound she heard was the whirring of the fan. Positive that she hadn't dreamed the noise, she slid out of bed and crept downstairs. Without turning on lights, she checked every window and door around the perimeter of the first floor. All were secure.

She must have been dreaming after all.

She glanced at the digital clock on the microwave and sighed. Only two o'clock, and she'd never get back to sleep. She decided to make a pot of coffee and resume reading about the evil slime that ate Maple Street. Maybe if she scared herself silly with fantasy, she wouldn't dwell on more dismal realities.

With no small amount of trepidation, Matt stared up at the oak tree. Its convoluted branches glowed in the moonlight, giving it a menacing appearance. He didn't bother to calculate the years it had been since he'd scaled a tree—he already knew it had been too long. He was beginning to think he should have waited until a decent hour to come back here. But once he'd reached a decision, he simply hadn't been able to wait another minute to see Hilary.

He stared up at the tree again. If Hilary could do it in the rain with pneumonia, then he could do it on a fine summer night in perfect health.

Once he reached the first branch, it wasn't so difficult, he decided, plotting his course up to Hilary's bedroom window. He shouldn't have given his set of house keys back to her, he reflected, pulling himself up to the next branch and ripping the sleeve of his shirt in the process. But he supposed it was too late to play "what if." There were a million things he'd done wrong where Hilary was concerned. Now the only thing that really mattered was setting a sure course for the future.

He allowed himself a sigh of relief as his feet touched the windowsill. The window was open and a box fan was wedged between the sill and the frame. No wonder Hilary hadn't heard him knocking at the front door, he mused. Not much could be heard over the clattering fan.

"Hilary?" he called out softly as he kept hold of the tree branch for balance with one hand and tried to open the window wider with the other, so he could move the fan and climb in. But the operation was awkward at best, and he ended up knocking the fan to the floor with a deafening crash.

"Hilary!" he called again, louder. "Don't be afraid, it's just me." As he climbed through the window, he could see she wasn't in her bed, but when he felt the sheets they were warm. She hadn't gone far. He set the fan upright and proceeded cautiously to the hallway.

The house was dark as he made his way down the stairs, with the exception of one light shining under the door to the kitchen. What was she doing awake at this hour? Matt wondered. And if she was awake, why hadn't she answered his knock at the front door?

It occurred to him then that perhaps she hadn't wanted to answer it. Maybe she didn't want a reconciliation. The thought numbed him with pain.

He pushed the kitchen door open. "Hil— Whoa!" The sound of an ear-piercing shriek alerted him to the cast-iron skillet bearing down on him. He swerved just in time to avoid a severe concussion.

"Matt?" Hilary blinked at him in confusion, the frying pan hanging limply from her hand. "Oh, my God, I thought you were the slime that ate Jenny Street. Did I hurt you?"

He grinned good-naturedly. "Not a bit. It was just a glancing blow. The slime that ate Jenny Street?"

"Or at the very least a burglar," she said with a shrug.

"Do you always dress like this for burglars?"

Hilary looked down at the creamy silk peignoir and blushed profusely. "No, dummy, I dressed like this for you. But you're a little late!"

Matt's grin faded. He reached out one hand and caught her chin, forcing her gaze into his. "You knew I was coming?"

"The roses knew, and they told me."

His smile returned. "So now they're talking back to you?"

"They certainly are. Matt, what are you doing here in the middle of the night?" She reached up to touch his bristly cheek. "And what is *this*?"

He felt his chin and grimaced. "I accidentally grew a beard, I guess. Bad idea, huh?"

Hilary took in the rest of him, then. His disheveled hair was badly in need of a trim, but that didn't stop her from wanting to run her fingers though it. His blue cotton shirt was torn, wrinkled and buttoned crookedly, and the sleeves were rolled up the elbow in unmatched, lumpy bunches. Only half of the shirttail was tucked in. And his jeans! They could walk by themselves. He was wearing one white sock and one blue sock, and the laces of his scuffed tennis shoes were secured in untidy knots.

"Matt, what happened to you?" she couldn't help asking.

For the first time, Matt became fully aware of his rumpled state. He hadn't given a thought to his clothes; he'd just thrown on the first thing handy, so great was his desire to rush here and put everything aright. How long had it been since he'd taken a shower? Lord, how could he expect Hilary to take him back when he looked and probably smelled something like a badly dressed bear?

"I fell in love, that's what happened to me," he finally answered, his voice low and achingly sincere. "It messed me up good, Hilary, but I'm learning to live with it."

She was moved beyond words. Unable to bear the distance between them any longer, she flew into his arms. He accepted her with a rumble of approval in his chest, holding her to him with the strength of at least two men his size.

"I'm sorry I made your life so miserable," she sobbed.

"No, oh, sweetheart no, you didn't do anything wrong. It was myself I had to fight."

"Then who won, you or yourself?" she asked with a sniff.

"We both did. I'm here with you, aren't I?" He pulled away from her so he could look into her eyes. "I wouldn't blame you if you threw me out, but... can I stay?"

"Yes." It was all she needed to say. Their mouths met hungrily, as if they'd been denied the right to kiss for hundreds of years. Hilary reveled in the familiar feel of his demanding lips on hers, familiar but somehow not quite the same—ah, the beard. The roughness added a new sensation to his kiss.

"Should I shave it?" he asked when she reached up to rub the whiskers.

"I'm not sure...it's certainly different," she answered diplomatically.

"I'll shave it," Matt said decisively. "And I desperately need a good long shower." He started to release her.

She held on tight. She was tempted by the thought of him fresh from a bath, smelling of soap and clean male skin, but right now she didn't want to let him go. "You can't just show up here and take a *shower*," she said.

"I know, I know, we need to talk."

She gave him her best come-hither look. "I had a lot more than talking in mind." When coyness didn't move him, she resorted to honesty. "I love you, Matthew Burke," she said softly. "I don't intend to let you leave me again, no matter what it is you have to say."

He fingered the satin edging of her peignoir, sending a wave of shivers coursing through her body. His expression grew serious—gravely so. "Nevertheless, I have to tell you something. I love you too, Hilary, more than I thought I could love anyone. But I want to get one thing straight before we...well, you might change your mind after I've had my say."

She gave him a guarded look that said, *Go ahead, do your worst.*

He gripped both of her shoulders in his strong hands. "I don't want you to have any illusions—I intend to marry you someday."

She opened her mouth in surprise, but he clamped a hand over it before she could speak.

"Now don't say anything yet. I know how you feel about marriage and getting tied down and all that stuff. But Hilary, I wouldn't expect you to be Donna Reed. You can go to Alaska and watch whales any time you damn well please, or you can go to New Zealand and watch penguins—I don't care. That is, I'll care, and I'll miss you if I can't go with you, but I won't try to stop you. And children—well, of course I'd love to have a couple or so, but that's entirely up to you. What I'm trying to say is I'd never tie you down."

His hand still covered her mouth, so she nipped his finger with her teeth. When he pulled his hand away in surprise, she gave him an expression of wide-eyed innocence. "Is that it?"

"Almost. I just want you to understand that it doesn't matter whether it's a year from now, or ten years from now, I'll wait until you're absolutely sure. But until then I'm going to do everything in my power to convince you that I'm the perfect husband for you. Now... go ahead, argue. I'm prepared."

Though her defenses should have sprung up at the mention of the word *marriage*, they didn't. Oddly enough, she didn't feel like arguing in the least. "Why don't you go take that shower?" she suggested. "I'd like a few moments to let this sink in."

"All right," he agreed a bit dazedly.

Hilary didn't have to think very hard. Her decision about marriage had already been made, though perhaps she was only just now acknowledging it. Two weeks without Matt had been enough to convince her that not only did she love him, but her world was utterly empty without him. She wanted to spend the rest of her life with him. Funny how the thought of all that permanence didn't disturb her in the slightest anymore. Now it was easy for her to picture herself as a wife, a good wife—Matt's wife.

When the bathroom door opened and a cloud of steam escaped, Hilary realized she'd been pacing the hallway, waiting for Matt to come out. "This has to be a record," she said, gazing appreciatively at his powerful body clad in only a towel. "You couldn't have been in there more than fifteen minutes."

"Twelve," he said with an embarrassed grin as he leaned against the door frame. "And that included a shave."

Hilary resisted the urge to touch his smooth cheek. When he reached for her, she took two steps backward, out of his grasp, and assumed an ultraserious expression. "Not so fast. I'm still not clear on this marriage stuff."

"What don't you understand?" His forehead wrinkled in concern.

"You mean I get to decide when, just as long as we do get married someday?" she asked, chewing thoughtfully on her lower lip.

He nodded. "Right."

"I could wait a year, or ten years, and you wouldn't mind?"

"If that's how long it takes."

She paused, as if she were deep in thought. "How do you feel about ten minutes?" she asked suddenly.

He gave her a blank look.

"Nah, on second thought I don't want to wait ten minutes. I've decided. Let's get married."

"What?" His voice cracked.

"Let's get married. Now. Tonight. We can fly to Reno. I can be dressed and have us packed in ten minutes. If you didn't bring any clothes with you, you left enough here to get by."

His brown eyes widened in disbelief. "Hilary, are you sure?"

She nodded, grinning confidently. "I've never been more sure about anything."

She didn't have to ask him again. He gave her a smile bright enough to blind her, then enveloped her in a hug that smelled of soap, toothpaste and menthol shaving cream. "You want to elope—that's the craziest, best thing I've heard in all my life. Just let me get dressed. Oh, and Hilary..."

"Yes?"

"Bring this silky thing with you, the robe and whatever's under it." He ran his hand along the gossamer fabric, from her hip to her shoulder and back again.

She laughed in sheer delight. As long as they'd waited to make love, they were going to postpone it again so they could get married. It was the best reason of all.

As they loaded her suitcase into the car a few minutes later in a fever of euphoria, Hilary remembered something important. "Before we leave, you have to see the roses," she told Matt, extracting a flashlight out of his glove compartment. She dragged him around the side of the house to the trellis by the garage, then shone the beam of light onto the rosebushes.

He stood speechless for at least a minute, just staring at the heavy clumps of blooms. "Well I'll be damned," he finally said, his voice touched with awe. "The roses *did* tell you I was coming, in their own way. Hilary, where are the garden shears?"

"They're right where they're supposed to be," she replied confidently. "But you aren't going to trim the bushes *now*, are you? Can't it wait?"

He was already headed for the greenhouse. "This absolutely cannot wait," he called over his shoulder. He turned on the light and found the shears hanging on a nail, right where they were supposed to be. In fact, every garden tool was clean and hanging or leaning in its proper place. Another small miracle.

With shears in hand, he returned to the rosebushes and cut a dozen just-opening flowers as Hilary held the light for him. She followed him as he took the cuttings into the house and watched, curious, as he wrapped the stems first in wet paper towels, then in plastic, and finally with some florist's tape.

When he was done he handed the flowers to her. "Your bride's bouquet."

She burst into joyful tears.

Three days later they rolled into their driveway at dawn, husband and wife in every sense of the word.

"We're home, Mrs. Burke—er, I mean, Ms. McShane," said Matt as he assisted a drowsy Hilary out of the front seat. He was still getting used to the fact that she wasn't going to change her name to his. But that was a small concession on his part, really, when he knew how much she valued her independence.

With his arms still around her shoulders, he opened the trunk and pulled out their suitcases, then slammed it shut again. He paused to gaze at the pink house. "I never fancied myself as an eccentric," he said. "What would you think of a nice gray?"

"It's always been pink," she said with definite huff in her voice, taking the overnight case he handed her. "Gray is dull."

"Then again, pink's all right," he said quickly as they made their way up the sidewalk. "Seriously, though, do you want to continue living here? We've discussed children, health insurance and retirement plans, but we haven't decided where to live. You haven't even seen my house in Blue Springs."

"Does it have central air and a hot tub?" she asked dreamily as he unlocked the front door. "I've always wanted those two things."

"Yup. But we could always add a few improvements to your house. And maybe a new coat of paint."

She halted halfway through the front door and glared at him.

"Pink, of course," he added.

"Of course." Her expression softened. "I'd like to consider living in your house, especially since you just had it remodeled. But right now I don't want to decide anything more important than which of my new nightgowns to put on. Really, Matt. I never pegged you for a sexy lingerie enthusiast."

He gave her a decadent smile. "I have many and varied interests aside from gardening and baseball."

"I'm looking forward to learning all about them." She wrapped her arms around him and nuzzled his neck.

He raised the hem of her emerald-green cotton blouse and placed his warm palm against the smooth skin of her back. "I don't much care which gown you wear," he whispered against her ear as he unbuttoned her blouse with his other hand. "I'll just peel it off of you."

"Then I won't bother with one," she said flippantly as she slid her blouse off her shoulders. They left a trail of clothing behind them as they made their way up the stairs, so that by the time they reached the bed they were gloriously naked.

Though they'd spent most of the past three days in bed, the newness of their intimacy had not worn off. Hilary suspected it never would. Each time they made love, it was a journey of discovery that ended with a feeling of having come home.

She'd been right about what would happen when Matt let go his control. His lovemaking was wildly creative, utterly untamed.

This time was no different. Matt coaxed her body to life with lingering caresses and bold kisses, leaving no part of her wanting for his touch. She explored him with equal thoroughness, running curious fingers over his hard chest, his flat stomach and all points north and south. When they were both breathless with excitement and could prolong it no further, he entered her warmth. She cried out from the sheer joy of it, and cried out again as they approached the delicious edge of ecstasy and then were catapulted beyond it.

Afterward they held each other with all the tenderness of a love hard fought for and won; Hilary sighed drowsily with the contentment of a woman utterly fulfilled. They slept curled around each other like puppies.

She wasn't sure how long they'd been dozing when the phone in the hall roused them. She started to get up, but Matt placed a possessive arm around her waist and held her fast.

"Let it ring," he said.

"It might be important," she insisted, untangling herself from the sheets. "We've been away for three days."

Reluctantly he let her go, then watched with appraising eyes as she flung her arms through the sleeves of a sheer robe. "If it's not a bona fide emergency, I want you back in this bed, pronto." He closed his eyes and listened to the soothing sound of her murmur as she talked on the phone.

"C'mon, Matt, get up and get dressed." Her voice nudged him out of a light sleep.

"What?"

"That was your aunt. She has something to show us, and it won't wait, she said."

"Like hell it won't wait. Did you tell her we'd been up all night?" Just the same, he did pull himself out of bed. Hilary's mysterious smile made him curious. She knew something she wasn't telling.

"Oh, yes. She has a few choice words to say about us eloping. But I won't paraphrase. I'll let Sheila tell you herself."

By the time they were dressed and headed out the front door, Matt's temperament had improved. He'd known his life with Hilary would be unpredictable. He had a feeling their marriage was starting out just the way it would continue—a crazy roller-coaster ride.

He reached over and ruffled Hilary's red-gold hair, still carelessly sleep-tousled. "What do you know about this mysterious thing Sheila dragged us out of bed for?" he asked.

"You'll have to wait and see it. But if it's what I think it is, you won't mind being dragged out of bed."

"Hah. It better be a live Sasquatch."

Sheila greeted them at the kitchen door with exuberant hugs and kisses. "You brats! How dare you get married without me! I had the wedding all planned out."

"I suppose you knew all along?" Matt asked with a skeptical tilt of his head.

"Of course I did." She wedged herself between them, then took them each by the hand and dragged them out the back door. "Come see this, and then you can fill me in on the gory details. You *do* have pictures, I hope?"

"Yes, the Chapel of Eternal Bliss had an excellent photographer," Hilary managed as she struggled to contain her laughter. They'd chosen the wedding chapel especially for its name.

But all laughter halted when they stopped at a spot in the garden. For a few moments, none of the three even breathed.

Sheila finally broke the silence. "Matt, Hilary, let me be the first to give you a wedding present," she said in a hushed voice, gesturing toward a scraggly bush next to the fence. The bush sported one fist-sized yellow bloom with an orange center, a burst of color that seemed to foreshadow good things to come.

* * * * *

SILHOUETTE'S "BIG WIN"
SWEEPSTAKES RULES & REGULATIONS
NO PURCHASE NECESSARY TO ENTER OR RECEIVE A PRIZE

1. To enter and join the Reader Service, scratch off the metallic strips on all your BIG WIN tickets #1-#6. This will reveal the values for each sweepstakes entry number, the number of free book(s) you will receive, and your free bonus gift as part of our Reader Service. If you do not wish to take advantage of our Reader Service, but wish to enter the Sweepstakes only, scratch off the metallic strips on your BIG WIN tickets #1-#4. Return your entire sheet of tickets intact. Incomplete and/or inaccurate entries are ineligible for that section or sections of prizes. Not responsible for mutilated or unreadable entries or inadvertent printing errors. Mechanically reproduced entries are null and void.

2. Whether you take advantage of this offer or not, your Sweepstakes numbers will be compared against a list of winning numbers generated at random by the computer. In the event that all prizes are not claimed by March 31, 1992, a random drawing will be held from all qualified entries received from March 30, 1990 to March 31, 1992, to award all unclaimed prizes. All cash prizes (Grand to Sixth), will be mailed to the winners and are payable by cheque in U.S. funds. Seventh prize to be shipped to winners via third-class mail. These prizes are in addition to any free, surprise or mystery gifts that might be offered. Versions of this sweepstakes with different prizes of approximate equal value may appear in other mailings or at retail outlets by Torstar Corp. and its affiliates.

3. The following prizes are awarded in this sweepstakes: ★ Grand Prize (1) $1,000,000; First Prize (1) $35,000; Second Prize (1) $10,000; Third Prize (5) $5,000; Fourth Prize (10) $1,000; Fifth Prize (100) $250; Sixth Prize (2500) $10; ★ ★ Seventh Prize (6000) $12.95 ARV.

   ★ This Sweepstakes contains a Grand Prize offering of $1,000,000 annuity. Winner will receive $33,333.33 a year for 30 years without interest totalling $1,000,000.

   ★ ★ Seventh Prize: A fully illustrated hardcover book published by Torstar Corp. Approximate value of the book is $12.95.

   Entrants may cancel the Reader Service at any time without cost or obligation to buy (see details in center insert card).

4. This promotion is being conducted under the supervision of Marden-Kane, Inc., an independent judging organization. By entering this Sweepstakes, each entrant accepts and agrees to be bound by these rules and the decisions of the judges, which shall be final and binding. Odds of winning in the random drawing are dependent upon the total number of entries received. Taxes, if any, are the sole responsibility of the winners. Prizes are nontransferable. All entries must be received by no later than 12:00 NOON, on March 31, 1992. The drawing for all unclaimed sweepstakes prizes will take place May 30, 1992, at 12:00 NOON, at the offices of Marden-Kane, Inc., Lake Success, New York.

5. This offer is open to residents of the U.S., the United Kingdom, France and Canada, 18 years or older except employees and their immediate family members of Torstar Corp., its affiliates, subsidiaries, Marden-Kane, Inc., and all other agencies and persons connected with conducting this Sweepstakes. All Federal, State and local laws apply. Void wherever prohibited or restricted by law. Any litigation respecting the conduct and awarding of a prize in this publicity contest may be submitted to the Régie des loteries et courses du Québec.

6. Winners will be notified by mail and may be required to execute an affidavit of eligibility and release which must be returned within 14 days after notification or, an alternative winner will be selected. Canadian winners will be required to correctly answer an arithmetical skill-testing question administered by mail which must be returned within a limited time. Winners consent to the use of their names, photographs and/or likenesses for advertising and publicity in conjunction with this and similar promotions without additional compensation.

7. For a list of major winners, send a stamped, self-addressed envelope to: WINNERS LIST, c/o MARDEN-KANE, INC., P.O. BOX 701, SAYREVILLE, NJ 08871. Winners Lists will be fulfilled after the May 30, 1992 drawing date.

If Sweepstakes entry form is missing, please print your name and address on a 3"×5" piece of plain paper and send to:

In the U.S.
Silhouette's "BIG WIN" Sweepstakes
901 Fuhrmann Blvd.
P.O. Box 1867
Buffalo, NY 14269-1867

In Canada
Silhouette's "BIG WIN" Sweepstakes
P.O. Box 609
Fort Erie, Ontario
L2A 5X3

Offer limited to one per household.

LTY-S790RR

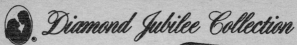

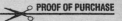